CW00474036

# A Diamond in the Dust

## The Stuarts: Love, Art and War

## Novel 1

**Michael Dean**

Holland Park Press London

Published by Holland Park Press 2022
Copyright © Michael Dean 2022

First Edition

The moral right of Michael Dean to be identified as the
author of this work has been asserted by hin in accordance
with the Copyright, Designs and Patents Act of 1988.

British Library Cataloguing-in-Publication Data
A catalogue record for this book is available from the British Library

ISBN 978-1-907320-96-5


Cover designed by Reactive Graphics

Printed and bound by
CPI Group (UK) Ltd, Croydon CR0 4YY

www.hollandparkpress.co.uk

*For Su and the girls, Jane and Rosie*

*With my own power my majesty they wound.*
*In the king's name the king himself they uncrown.*
*So does the dust destroy the diamond.*

Verse attributed to Charles I

# PROLOGUE
## THE STUARTS: LOVE, ART AND WAR

Charles Stuart, the captain of his guard, Colonel Francis Hacker, and just two halberdiers made their way toward the scaffold where Charles was to be executed. The little procession came first to the Bear Gallery at Whitehall Palace. Charles could conjure up every one of the thirty-five paintings which had hung there.

Those blank spaces on the now grimy walls had once hosted some of the greatest portraits ever painted, including three by van Dyck. As Charles recalled, the van Dyck image of the poet Sir John Suckling had carried the motto 'Do not look for yourself outside yourself'.

What better motto for any man with the soul of an artist, whether he practised the arts or not? And where is the good Suckling now? That loyal royalist who had fought so nobly for him. Was he alive or dead? Would he, Charles Stuart, King of England no more, soon be joining him in heaven?

And here had been van Dyck's painting of Inigo Jones, master architect. If he was alive, he would be a very old man by now. Inigo had come a long way, in time and place from Charles's mother's court in Denmark via Italy to here. Blessings on his devoted aged head.

They moved on to the Adam and Eve Stairs Room where there had once been twenty-four paintings. Charles stopped in front of a white space in the grime on the wall. He looked apprehensively round at Colonel Hacker, who nodded permission.

The painting which had hung here was something of a curio. It had been entered in the inventory as *Charles I With The Queen and Court at Greenwich*. It showed no fewer than thirteen figures and a dog in a wavy line on a hill at Greenwich, disporting in the open air.

Jan van Belcamp had limned the figures. He was the only man of the arts to betray him and work for the Puritan destroyers.

Charles and his small party walked on to the Privy Gallery, which had been a more public place. It still was, it would seem, as a few soldiers passed him by without taking any great interest. He came to a halt with a start. There were tulip-wood tables placed along the walls with pictures stacked on them, some propped flat up, some facing flat down, some on their sides, all piled up anyhow.

His eye was caught by the van Dyck of himself, black-armoured on horseback, with M de St Antoine holding his helmet at the horse's side. His face relaxed to a near smile at the sight of the gnarled, tough little riding master, an old man even then; red hair, red beard, bright red suit and riding boots.

The portrait was upside down; face up on top of a pile of other paintings. It was also grubby with neglect and the frame was cracked.

Charles gave a start and a kind of mewing cry. Some of the pictures had price tags and thumbnail descriptions. There was the portrait of Nicholas Lanier. The carved gilt frame was cracked in two places. Painted in Antwerp by a very young van Dyck, it had once hung in the Bear Gallery. Nicholas Lanier, Master of the King's Music, that benevolent smiling soul. 'How are your family, Nicholas? They always meant so much to you.'

'Nicholas Lanier, half a figure', said the description on the tag, copied from the inventory. Abraham van der Doort had entered these words, in his usual slipshod way, in *A Catalogue and Description Of King Charles The First's Capital Collection Of Pictures, Limnings, Statues, Bronzes, Medals, And Other Curiosities.*

Charles turned the description over and read the price tag. It was on sale for £10, a tenth of the price of a van Dyck in his pomp. Charles winced at the coarsening of the genius's memory.

Where was Nicholas Lanier now? Had he been at the siege with the other men of art? Charles could no longer remember. Inigo had been there. Wat Montagu was in the Tower, that Charles did know. So many true good men, all scattered, some gone.

One painting was on the floor, face down. It had been badly used. It looked as if someone had trodden on it. It was William Dobson's portrait of Endymion Porter, painted at Oxford. Charles clenched his fists and groaned. England's greatest painter so sorely abused. And Endymion abused with him, now fled to France when they seized his house in the Strand.

They entered the Banqueting House, one of the wonders of the western world, planned and designed by Inigo Jones. A middle window had been crudely hacked out, converted to a door through which Charles was to pass to the scaffold. The Banqueting House was to be his last sight on earth, before the executioner swung his axe. Cromwell had planned it so.

As he stepped into the mighty hall, Charles started to shake with rage. The place was filthy. Two cavalry regiments had been stationed here. Horse manure was trampled into the floor and the walls were thick with grime.

But an even bigger shock was the crude wooden partitions, making makeshift rooms from the massy hall. The partitions ruined the proportions of the Banqueting House which had hosted the glorious masques on Twelfth Night or Shrove Tuesday. The masques which sought to reflect the same harmony, proportion and beauty as the Banqueting House which staged them.

He breathed hard for a moment then steeled himself to look up at the Banqueting House ceiling. This is what Oliver Cromwell had intended. He may be doing Cromwell's will, but his thoughts were his own. That, at least, could not be taken from him.

Charles's gaze went to the panel next to King James's apotheosis, his father's ascent to heaven. Minerva is shown, representing heroic chastity and destroying lust. At this, Minerva had done a pretty poor job with James.

Charles took one final look at his father ascending to heaven, blocked out by Inigo Jones and expensively coloured by Rubens, then walked through the window, out to his execution.

At the moment Charles was beheaded, the statue of him by Hubert Le Sueur at the Old Exchange also had its head cut off by the mob.

# CONTENTS

# CHAPTER 1
## *THE STING OF THE THORN*

Charles Stuart's first memory of his life upon this earth was pain. There was pain all over his body, though it was worse in his legs, his feet and his back. It never completely disappeared.

His sister, Elizabeth, four years older, told him of his birth, to show him how far he had come to overcome such a start. In the gloomy depths of November, 1600, he was born in Dunfermline Palace, in Scotland. His father, James, had given Dunfermline Palace to his mother, Anne of Denmark, as a wedding present. James was there when Charles was born, but only because he had fled the plague in Edinburgh.

The precocious Elizabeth had assisted at the birth. She told Charles, with a wry smile, that the midwife had screamed at the sight of this undersized, twisted apparition, like a red shell-less crab. She had sent out for the Chamberlain, Henry Wardlaw, to fetch James.

James blanched. It was clear to him that baby Charles had some of the very afflictions he suffered from himself, though in even worse form. It was if the boy's skeleton were made of candle wax not bone. It bent, it flopped about. The weight of it bowed the legs and left the spine curved.

James fled from the lifelong reminder of his own curse. A reminder that was to become even worse when Charles spoke, as the spluttering, near-incomprehensible speech was again reminiscent of James, only worse.

A hasty baptism was arranged by the Chamberlain at James's command, before Charles expired. His mother remained in bed, too weak to do more than weep. An astrologer was called, one Charles Kinloch, who fled the room after one glance at the baby and presumably his fate.

A distinctly unenthusiastic three-gun salute was ordered which rang out from the battlements over the 'pend' as it was called, the driveway which ran through the park, then through the basement of Dunfermline Palace.

Charles's memory of the day his parents left Dunfermline Palace, some three years after he was born, was of a thunderous rap on the palace gates with a staff, then a breathless messenger from England telling the assembled court that Queen Elizabeth was dead. James was king now not only of Scotland but of England and Ireland as well.

As Charles's sister patiently explained to him, this memory was undoubtedly the product of Charles's vividly-coloured pictorial imagination. But leave his parents did, along with his brother, Henry, though not the ever-devoted Elizabeth.

James left behind instructions to a physician, Dr Henry Atkins: The wretched boy's tongue-tie was to be cured by cutting; his bow-legs were to be straightened by strapping them into iron boots; his body was to be pulled straight by a tight corset and he was to be fed on a diet of curds and whey because his decayed teeth did not permit of chewing. Dr Atkins was given £100 and told to send regular reports on Charles, which James never read.

The toddler Charles was alone in the massive gloom of the palace, except for Elizabeth and the palace staff who all came in to talk to him and play with him. He quickly grew fond of them.

There was the Keeper, John Gibb, the gardener, John Lowrie, the plumber, James Coupar, who took the toddler with him when he fixed the lead roofs, and there was Thomas Walwood, the foreman of the coal pits who gave the delighted child coal to play with.

And at least one of his birth problems was lessened by the servants: They could understand his thick Scottish accent through the tied-tongue. But the problem of his other afflictions remained. If pain was his first feeling in life, his first reasoning was the never-ending battle to understand why he had been so afflicted. How had he displeased God so?

He was plagued, tortured, by the idea that those fair of form and face are also virtuous and have been made so by God. Those maimed of form and ugly have displeased God. The soul is born in the womb and is a reflection of the body. A deformed body means a deformed soul. Even his fox-coloured hair, again reminiscent of James, to his father's disgust, surely showed God's curse on him.

Twenty years later, Charles was able to name his main affliction. A practitioner of physic called John Rickets of Newberry had been treating children with twisted bodies and small bowed legs. He named their affliction after himself – rickets.

But before that, in the damp gloom of Dunfermline Palace, the toddler who could hardly toddle found a balm close at hand.

Charles's sister, Elizabeth Stuart, had been named for Gloriana – Queen Elizabeth, the greatest monarch in English history, as everybody said. The saviour of the Protestant faith. Elizabeth Stuart seemed like a little adult to Charles; every bit as glorious as Gloriana. There she was, sweet and serious in her tight blue taffeta bodice, pulled demurely high, her little pointed stomacher and her modest plain skirt, worn wide over a farthingale to push it out.

Charles did not look all that different from her. He wore a long skirt to hide his deformed legs, with a tight padded doublet and lace ruff. Thus attired, he faced his sister, who with gritted teeth and spleen worthy of her namesake set out to cure her little brother of all ailments.

She started with the stutter. She prevailed on Dr Atkins not to cut his tongue. At Elizabeth's suggestion, Atkins, ever the diplomat, simply ignored the issue when reporting to James.

Elizabeth had noticed that Charles did not stutter when he sang. Charles loved singing and not only singing songs. He could imitate instruments with his high voice, and loved doing so. Henry Wardlaw could play the viola passably and John Gibb could play the lute. Charles sang along with them, beautifully, fluently...

The same principle of following nature not breaking it was applied by Elizabeth to her brother's inability to walk. She persuaded the doctor not to fix leg irons to his legs, but instead got Henry Wardlaw to send to London for stiff leather boots with brass inserts. These supported his ankle joints, which still had not knitted together properly.

The precocious Elizabeth believed that if the ankles were held in the correct position and supported, the knee and even the hip joints, which also had not knitted properly, would have a chance to do so.

But as with the stutter, her breakthrough came by observing little Charles closely. She watched him in his skirt, struggling to walk. He walked better on tippy-toe. Strangely, he could run on tippy-toe better than he could walk. And he could dance even more easily than he could run or walk.

There followed days of unexpected happiness for Charles and Elizabeth. In the morning, there was a bath for Charles with sweet water and a mixture of herbs. Every afternoon there was music, at first provided by Wardlaw and Gibb alone, then by musicians they hired.

They put together a consort of viols, treble tenor and bass, sometimes also with a violin. As they played, Charles danced and sang to the music with Elizabeth banging out the rhythm with a stick. They sang and danced to Byrd and Dowland but a particular favourite of Charles's was Orlando Gibbons, especially his *See, the Word Is Incarnate*.

Elizabeth banged the rhythm, Charles on tippy-toe danced and tried to sing at the same time.

SEE, the WORD is in CARnate.
GOD is made MAN in the WOMB of a VIRgin.
SHEPherds rejoice
Wise MEN aDORE and anGELS sing.
GLOry be to GOD on high: PEACE on EARTH.

Even when he fell, collapsing in a heap on the floor, Charles burst out in giggling laughter:

'Elizabeth, I love you!'

'I love you, too,' the solemn little adult-child replied.

She was nine years old at the time and had afflictions of her own. She was prone to sudden violent nosebleeds which took a frightening time to stop. Sometimes, the dancing came to a sudden end, then the floor would be wiped of her blood.

Charles slowly came to terms with the wreck of his body. He came to understand that God was dealing with him as He did with St Paul, not removing the thorn, yet making His grace sufficient to take away the sting of it.

## CHAPTER 2
## *THE GREAT PRINCE*

Charles was finally deemed old enough to join the rest of the family in England, but his parents had neglected to arrange a bed for him on his first night in London. His older brother, Prince Henry, the heir to the throne, gave up his lodgings in Whitehall so Charles had somewhere to lay his head.

Charles would have slept on the floor at Henry's feet, had he been allowed to. Henry was more like a God than a man; at least, he was to Charles. He was the radiant sun of the English hemisphere.

Charles forever pictured Henry at the barriers. The barriers staged mock battles to discover where true virtue triumphed most. And there was Henry, armed with two swords, defending his barrier with eight knights against a mock attack by over fifty challengers.

Henry always called Charles 'the bishop' as his bent and bandy legs could be hidden only by a bishop's surplice. Charles giggled at the nickname the first time he heard it, and revelled in it after that. It was a fond warm teasing from the sun on high. He had, after all, once written to Henry from Scotland imploring his older brother to 'love me'.

Charles watched and applauded Henry at the tiltyard; wielding the pike, shooting with the bow, leaping, vaulting. Then there was Henry mastering foreign policy, so he could advance the Protestant cause when he became king. He corresponded in French with his godfather Henri IV of France, who had led the French Huguenots in the Civil War.

Henri IV had sent our Prince Henry armour, pistols and a sword as well as his own riding instructor, M de St Antoine, who had also taught Charles the art of riding, and riding with shield and sword. The French king had been arming Henry for righteous battle against the Catholics when he was assassinated for his beliefs.

And then there was Henry the lover, youth though he still was, charming the beautiful young Frances Howard, Countess of Essex. It was a pure love Henry had with Frances, the antithesis of his father's dissolute life.

Henry reacted to that not only by loving purely but by drinking and eating moderately – with fruit his only innocent passion – and insisting on a swear box to fine those using bad language. Henry was building himself into a rounded and perfect renaissance prince.

He was also brave enough to defy James, which was brave indeed, as James could be brutal. As his first experience of London, days after he arrived, James had sent Charles to the Tower to see a bear which had mauled a child being eaten by lions. The message was clear. Disobedience would be followed by punishment.

But James, like everybody else, adored Henry, even when Henry defied him. He was blazingly defiant of his father over James's imprisonment of the great adventurer from Elizabeth's time, Raleigh. Charles remembered Henry, white in the face, fists clenched, as he ground out, 'Surely, no king but our father would keep such a bird in a cage.'

Raleigh had been in the Tower since his reprieve from the scaffold, accused of trying to put Arabella Stuart on the throne instead of James, when Elizabeth died. Henry's well-developed sense of justice was aroused. To him, Raleigh was a poet, a great sailor and privateer and a great Englishman.

Henry visited Raleigh regularly in prison to James's gibbering fury. He brought him gifts and had his prison conditions improved, in public defiance of James. He even consulted Raleigh when he commissioned the recently launched *Prince Royal*, a massive warship. Henry worked directly with Raleigh and Phineas Pett, the King's Master Shipwright. It was weeks before James even found out about it.

## CHAPTER 3
### *A PICTURE WITH LIGHT AND MOTION*

Charles had no memories of his mother during his childhood in Scotland, but after the move to London he visited her as often he could at her residence in Denmark House, in the Strand. Sometimes she refused to see him.

On this occasion, a late May Day, he had travelled the short distance from Whitehall Palace not by river, as he usually did, but by royal carriage. Most people could have walked it, but Charles still found walking more difficult than dancing or riding.

So Charles approached Denmark House from the front, not the back as he would have done had he arrived by river, and unconsciously frowned at the Tudor higgledy-piggledy of the building. He was received by his mother in the Receiving Room which, typically, had been built at the end of the east wing, inconveniently far from Anne's quarters.

The Receiving Room was a richly painted, marbled and gilded room in white gold and blue. Charles's heart leapt as his mother greeted him with unaccustomed warmth and even a touch of energy. She was enthroned in a winged armchair in front of the Chimney Piece, with her medicinal herbs on an oak side table next to her. There were blue borage flowers to lift her sadness and there was hellebore to ease her gout.

'Charles. Daarlink. Sit down. Speak with me.'

Anne had never lost her Danish accent. Her English was actually getting worse as she retreated further and further from James.

Charles sat in a high-backed, carved wooden chair, beaming at his mother. She was a pretty woman, everybody thought so – except her husband. She had an oval face, like Henry and Charles himself, with a jaunty pointy nose, intelligent high forehead and bright grey-blue eyes. She rejected the fashionable low-cut dresses, not only today when she was receiving her son, but on all her rare appearances in public. At times she wore a black manta-style headdress to display her Catholic faith.

Unusually, his mother took the conversational initiative, 'Look at this daarlink. Mr Jones made it for me to wear on *Tethys Festival*. He is making all the costumes and headdresses as well as the settings for the masque.'

She waved at her maid to bring forward the headdress which had been placed on a table, and show it to Charles. Plumed with ostrich feathers and with a long gauze train pinned to it, the headdress was indeed a thing of wonder.

'You see? Mr Inigo Jones has made seashells and pearls for my hair,' said Anne, delightedly.

'It's beautiful, mamma!' Charles meant it.

Anne cackled. 'Lady Arundel will be très très jealous from me. She dances the Nymph of Trent.'

Charles nodded absently, away with his own thoughts. He knew his mother was dancing the part of Tethys, Queen of the Ocean and wife of Neptune. He glanced at her rare half-smile, realising that dancing gave her the only pleasure she had. She often spoke of dancing in a Ben Jonson masque, the *Masque of Blackness*, many years ago, alongside all the ladies of her court. Inigo Jones had created the tableau. It was the happiest moment of her life.

Anne was stroking the seashells and pearls of her headdress as if they were alive. 'I brought Inigo here, you know,' Anne said. Charles did know, Anne had said so, dreamily, many times. 'He was at my brother King Christian's court in Copenhagen. He lived like a monk and worked and worked. Before that he studied Palladio in Rome. Lady Arundel takes credit for him because her husband was his patron but I told Christian about him. I brought him here from Denmark with me, when I was fifteen. He belongs to *me*. He is *mine*.'

Charles nodded absently, half listening. He was about to tell his mother his secret, the reason for his visit. But with a sudden spurt of excitement he changed his mind. He would keep his secret secret. He would clutch it to him. Without being aware of it, he folded his arms round himself, folding himself inside himself.

His big secret was that he, Charles Stuart, was dancing in *Tethys Festival*, too. Elizabeth, most darling of sisters, had helped him rehearse, hour after hour since early in March. His mother did not think he could do it, on his bandy legs, but he would surprise her.

They had arranged a group of well-born maidens to dance round him, to hide his legs, but he intended to dance free of them, at the performance. He intended to dance alone on the stage, out there in front of his mother. He intended to shine. He intended to soar as far as the sun.

He intended to make his mother love him and never leave him again.

*Tethys Festival* was a masque to be shown at the Banqueting House, in Whitehall Palace. It was to celebrate Henry becoming Prince of Wales, the Lord of the Isles, the formal successor to the realm of James. It would show Tethys, Queen of the Ocean and wife of Neptune, diverting all the rivers to the new Prince of Wales, the new Lord of the Isles.

On this balmy bee-filled day of days there was no cloud in God's truth of a sky outside. The only clouds were from Inigo Jones's cloud machines above the painting of a port, the first backdrop. But Inigo's clouds could change shape at the behest of man, thanks to his ingenious systems of pulleys and slats.

The ambassadors and notables had been told to arrive at four o'clock. There were mutterings behind gloved hands about this. *Tethys Festival* was to last less than an hour. The king himself had announced that he would not be appearing until six, when the masque could start. There would be a lot of empty time spent idly waiting.

Even more contentious were the seating arrangements. At the courts of Spain and France, these would be the subject of lavish protocol, worked on for weeks by the monarch's household staff, led by the Groom of the Chamber.

In James's case, the seating, as with much else, had been subordinated to his lusts. The Venetian Ambassador, Nicolo Molinò along with the Spanish Ambassador, Gaspar de Guzmán, Count Olivares, had been allotted high-born women who they were permitted, even encouraged, to fondle during the performance.

Within James's all-consuming need for debauchery was a smaller but no less sharp taste for public debauchery, especially during open occasions like entertainments. Henry's friend, Frances Howard, Countess of Essex, a full-breasted beauty of sharp intelligence and no little wit, had been told to make herself available to Olivares. Fashionable necklines were very low anyway, but it had been made clear to Frances Howard that her bosom should be naked or near naked for Olivares's pleasure.

James was especially in thrall to the Spanish Ambassador as Olivares sent his minions into the stews of St Giles to procure boys for the king. That was the basis of his much gossiped about hold over James. James himself, meanwhile, would be seated at the masque with his current favourite, or 'master-mistress' as he sometimes called him, the blonde womanly-looking Robert Carr, who James had brought with him from Scotland.

James always had one favourite on the go who he could take to his bed every night to express adoration in baby-talk with slobbered kisses. Favour was further shown by the granting of titles and lands.

Among the lands given to the current favourite, Robert Carr, were those in Dorset belonging to Sir Walter Raleigh, still languishing in the Tower. Raleigh's pleading letters to

Carr and to James not to send his wife and children out into the streets were ignored.

Finally, in early evening, with the audience on three sides of the stage, the masque began. The traverse serving as a curtain with its dark clouds and sparkling stars moved as the music struck up from in front of the stage. The music was by Orlando Gibbons, the organist at the Chapel Royal and Charles and Elizabeth's childhood favourite from their days at Dunfermline Palace.

As the traverse was slowly drawn back, a statue of Neptune was revealed before the port of Milford Haven. Prince Henry appeared as Lord of the Isles, dressed from head to toe in green, with black shoes. Behind him came William Cavendish, a close friend the same age, playing the part of Triton, surrounded by an honour guard of lesser tritons. All the tritons were dressed in skin-coats of watchet – light blue – taffeta lightened with silver to show the muscles of their bodies.

William Cavendish presented the sword of Astrea – goddess of justice – to Henry:

*And there withal she wills him greet the Lord*
*And Prince of the Isles, the hope and the delight*
*Of all the northern nations.*

Inigo Jones was standing to one side, in the shadows. He tensed as the first test of his machinery drew near. The tableau changed from the port to a grotto; all the slats of the moving scenery moved smoothly. Queen Tethys was discovered in the grotto, seated on a rock. In *The Masque of Blackness* Anne had been lowered from a cloud, but that was five years ago. These days she had become rather more portly, her legs and stomach were swelling. Inigo did not want to chance it.

Anne waved languidly to the audience as the slats parted to reveal her. She did not regard herself as playing a part, as if this were a play in the theatre. She saw herself as exalting her own majesty and by reflection the majesty of the crown in general. The watchers gasped, many applauded. Inigo Jones gave a windy sigh, then belched. His guts were tighter than a violin string playing a gavotte.

The next test was the change of scene when the Queen vanishes, having given her blessing, and the tableau changes to one of whales and sea horses. This was achieved. The musicians, on a raised dais at the same level as the stage, struck up a galliard.

Charles was now to appear as Zephyrus, the west wind, calling up the rivers to bless Henry's future reign as Henry IX which everybody in the Banqueting House knew would be a glorious time.

As Zephyrus, Charles wore a brief robe of green satin with silver wings, an aureole of finest lawn and a floral garland. Around him, the 'six of high descent' in the text by Samuel Daniel were all naiads, river goddesses with coral and shells in their hair, seaweed hanging from their shoulders and crescent moons trimming the upper part of their diaphanous skirts.

Each naiad, dancing a galliard around Charles to hide his bandy legs, represented a different river, flowing to bless Henry's reign. His sister Elizabeth danced the nymph of Arun, Lady Arabella Stuart danced the nymph of Trent, the Countess of Derby danced the nymph of Derwent, the countess of Dorset the nymph of Ayr, Lady Elizabeth Grey the nymph of Medway and Frances Howard, Countess of Essex danced the nymph of Lee, representing the River Lea in Essex.

There was a mighty bellowing roar from the front of the audience. King James broke off from his ministrations of Robert Carr.

'What the buggery is she doing there?' James turned furiously on his seat, trying to locate Olivares, presumably sitting alone having been deprived of his prey in the shape of Frances Howard.

Frances, one of the shrewdest women in London as well as one of the cleverest, had applied to Inigo to dance in the masque as soon as she had discovered James's intentions for her. Inigo knew nothing of James's plans and granted the high-born lady's wishes immediately.

The dancing slowed at the king's rage, then came to a halt. James stood up. He bellowed again. Charles realised his father was very drunk. He looked for his mother, but since ascending to heaven on one of Inigo's clouds she had disappeared. She had not seen even the start of his dance, which had stopped now in any case. Elizabeth moved next to Charles and squeezed his arm. She whispered in his ear. 'Never mind!'

Henry seized the moment and took centre stage, every inch the future king. The audience hushed and hung on his words. He spoke Samuel Daniel's lines with a passion:

*Pleasures only shadows be*
*Cast by bodies we conceive,*
*And are made the things we deem*
*In those figures which they seem.*
*But those pleasures vanish fast*
*Which by shadows are expressed;*
*Pleasures are not if they last;*
*In their passing is their best.*

# CHAPTER 4
## THE GREATEST OF THE KINGLY RACE IS GONE

Charles was happily aware that his adored older sister was flowering into a beauteous young woman. Every Protestant prince in Europe was touted as a suitor, but in Charles's mind and Henry's and fortunately in James's, too, one young prince was the obvious candidate to unify the Protestant kingdoms in a marriage alliance, Henry's friend since childhood, Frederick – Frederick V of the Palatinate.

An enthusiastic Frederick had seen a copy of Robert Peake's portrait of Elizabeth – oval face, fine features, long elegant figure – and had read Henry's accounts of his sister's virtues and talents. She even liked hunting, a passion Frederick shared with James.

On arrival for his nuptials in London, Frederick was rowed up the Thames in state and was met at Westminster Steps by Charles.

'Ach, die Englische Krankheit,' said Frederick, nodding at Charles's bandy legs and twisted torso.

Charles knew that rickets was called 'the English disease' in Frederick's native German. Far from taking offence, he burst out laughing. Frederick gave him a bear-hug which left him breathless and the two of them were like brothers before Frederick had taken more than half a dozen steps on land.

Frederick's popularity spread well beyond Charles and the court. A play by Wentworth Smith entitled *The Hector of Germany* lauded Elizabeth's heroic new husband as the saviour of Protestantism. Charles asked Henry to take him to see it, but Henry was busy arranging the wedding, not to mention running the realm, so he asked his friend William Cavendish to take young Charles to the performance and look after him.

The play was on for one night at the Red Bull. It was also staged at the Curtain, but Charles chose the Red Bull, in Clerkenwell, which he had heard was rowdier, being right near the exotic-sounding stews of Smithfield. William Cavendish, with all the grave authority of a seventeen-year-old, told Charles the Red Bull could hold three thousand five hundred people, far more than the Curtain, which made it more important.

If anything, there were even more there when Charles and William arrived. The place was heaving to the eaves with excited theatregoers, the largest assembly Charles had ever seen in all his twelve years.

Charles suddenly thought with warmth of Inigo Jones, who had been brought up right near here, in Smithfield. Charles knew Inigo's family had lived in penury, always going hungry. His reverie was interrupted by a commentary on the scene before them by William Cavendish.

'This place usually offers rope acts and such public entertainments, drolleries and so forth,' Cavendish was explaining loftily, as he and Charles sat unnoticed in the Gods, among the sinful sixpenny mechanics, as William laughingly and dangerously loudly called them.

'Have you never been before?'

'N... n... no.'

'O just follow my lead. I'll tell you what to do. And I shall explain the Cockney dialect to you as it goes along, if you wish it.'

'Thank you, William.'

'And there are fights during the performances, on occasion. But I shall protect you.'

'Thank you, William.'

Remarkably, to Charles, this was an amateur production in a public playhouse, something he had not heard of before and did not think was possible – a citizens' play. The citizen actors were apprentices and shopkeepers, Charles even recognised one of the stall-holders from the stalls round the walls of Whitehall. Such people thought so highly of Frederick they had put on this play in his honour. That was wonderful.

Charles joined in the whooping and hollering as actors wandered onto the stage in the clothes they usually wore, and Wentworth Smith's play began. It depicted the newly arrived Frederick as the Black Prince.

Frederick as the Black Prince was called the Palsgrave, meaning his title, Elector of the Palatinate. The Palsgrave's identification as Frederick was signalled broadly when the character received the Order of the Garter, as Frederick was soon to do from James. The audience gave whoops of recognition at the depiction of this well-known and much anticipated event. The actors stopped acting to take well-deserved bows and smile and wave at the audience.

Set in medieval Germany, the Hector of Germany compared Frederick's hoped-for attacks on Catholic Spain with a campaign by the Black Prince in Spain, which may or may not have actually taken place. To cheers from the audience, including the two well-born boys, the Palsgrave announces his inspirational predecessor:

> Here in Spain where the Black Prince encamped
> And made the bastard flee.

Then Spanish assassins are sent to England. This was shown by a stallholder strutting the stage high-kneed in a Spanish style beard with a pocket-dag in his hand, to jeers and boos from the audience. These pocket-dags were pocket pistols, much identified with Spanish assassins. Rumours were sweeping London that the Jesuits had sent assassins to kill Frederick or Henry or both of them.

An ineffectual, wheezing, middle-aged figure came onto the stage. He lumbered after a wooden cut-out stag before flapping at the Jesuit assassins. The audience recognised King James, who was greeted with whoops of derision. Charles and William Cavendish looked at each other, then joined in.

Charles slept in the royal carriage on the way back to Whitehall. That evening at the play with William Cavendish was the happiest in all his boyhood.

The betrothal was at the Banqueting House at Whitehall the following evening, on a crisp late autumn day. The atmosphere was warmed considerably by the prospective bride and groom taking one look at each other and being transported by love. Elizabeth took his broad shoulders and even the smallpox scarred skin as the epitome of manhood. Other people fell away. To the end of their time on earth, Elizabeth and Frederick could remember nothing about that day, except each other.

On the excuse of showing him his own portrait in the Bear Gallery, painted by van Mierevelt, Elizabeth led him away, taking him by the hand. They stopped in front of the van Mierevelt portrait.

'He provided the ruff, it wasn't my idea.' Frederick laughed, pretending indignation at the starched ruff sticking out on either side of his chin like a stopping place for small birds. 'God's teeth, why on earth are you trying to get this Mierevelt fellow over here?' Frederick continued, talking through his laughter. 'The man has not the first idea of how to render his subject. I am much better looking than that.'

Elizabeth was smiling. 'Yes,' she said, 'you are.' And then, with brazen confidence. 'Much better looking.'

'But I am but a frog compared to you, my princess.'

'Indeed.' She pulled him into an anteroom and they talked for three hours. Elizabeth sent a footman to say they were not to be disturbed. She spoke lovingly of her brothers: How brave Charles was in his affliction. How he prayed not to be cured but to bear God's burden on him with humility. She told Frederick how artistic he was, how shrewd his judgements of the arts. Charles, she said, was a pure and sensitive soul.

Frederick said he felt Henry was already his brother, too, and had been so throughout the years of their correspondence. But Elizabeth laughingly told him of Henry's 'feet of clay'.

He had an over-broad sense of mischief and would surely try to lead Frederick into trouble. And when he gambled his usually sound judgement faltered.

Frederick, in his turn, spoke seriously of his sense of mission to build a Protestant alliance. It was not some political convenience, he said, flushing with passion. Roman Catholicism was mysticism. It interposed itself between man and his Christ. It set out to confuse, bamboozle and dazzle honest peasants and yeomen into submission.

Elizabeth was nodding solemnly. She agreed, broadly, but felt his passion inside her, heating her own. The passion could have been about anything. His desires became her desires as he talked. Before the evening was out she had told her ladies-in-waiting, none too secretively, to admit him to her chamber if he appeared. He did.

Festivities and honours followed. As already celebrated in Wentworth Smith's play, Frederick received the Order of the Garter. This was highly unusual, because he was a foreigner. Not only that, he was invested in the Order in a private ceremony conducted by James himself, with Charles happily attending. An orange and tawny ribbon could now be worn on Frederick's doublet forever, to mark the honour. After the ceremony, to show his delight with his new son-in-law, James took Frederick into his private bedchamber and presented him with a valuable ring.

Elizabeth beamed at him proudly. She was a picture of bliss and beauty in a blue silk gown from London's master mercer, Benjamin Henshawe, richly decorated with gold and silver lace.

Next day, there was a mock sea battle on the Thames at Whitehall. There were floating castles with fireworks. Phineas Pett, the King's Master Shipwright, was made to take part as captain of a tiny pinnace of the King's, a little ship called *The Spy*.

Phineas was made to stand on deck, proudly at command, while Frederick and Henry fired cannon at him from the shore, roaring with laughter. Phineas stayed bravely at his post, perhaps fortified by Henry's recent saving of his career and probably his life when he was unjustly accused of profiteering on materials for the king's ships.

That evening, there was a banquet at the Guildhall for Frederick and Elizabeth hosted by the new Lord Mayor of London, Sir John Swinnerton. It was attended by representatives of the German and Dutch nobility accompanying Frederick, sealing the Protestant union. Frederick was showered with gifts. The court guards and messengers had opulent new liveries of red cloth embroidered with the king's initials and an imperial crown studded with gold.

Anne did not attend the banquet, pleading swellings and pains in her legs. She was known to be against the match, alleging that she would have preferred a Catholic prince and perhaps a Spanish alliance, instead. But her absence was hardly noticed; her objections brushed aside.

One reason for the indifference towards Anne was a perturbing and highly unusual occurrence, which took place during the banquet, overshadowing everything else. Henry was taken ill. He sweated profusely, vomited, then fainted.

He took to his bed, for the first time in his life. Still in high fever, he struggled out for the Lord Mayor's pageant, a glorious procession arranged by Thomas Dekker, the playwright. But he collapsed again and had to be borne back to his bed, worse than before. He was taken to the quietude of Oatlands Palace, in Surrey, as if the silence would help nurse him.

The diagnosis was a tertian ague, a hot and cold choler known as yellow bile. A great shaking came over Henry, he was subject to cold fits then hot. He could not swallow; liquids were poured down his throat from a syrup jar but he brought them back again immediately. His mind was possessed by ravings. Some connected all this with a swim in the Thames the day before Henry was taken ill, but the causal chain was not clear.

Naturally, physicians were called, many of them, including Dr William Butler, the celebrated physician of Cambridge. A concerned James sent his personal physician, the Leiden trained Sir William Paddy. Some of them wanted more bleeding, and purging, some wanted bleeding and purging stopped, as Henry was too weak for it. Endless conferences were held among the medical men.

The festivities for Frederick and Elizabeth's wedding were put on hold. James continued to go out hunting because he had no idea what else to do with his days. Anne took to her bed. A lunar rainbow appeared over Oatlands, a dreadful omen.

By now Henry was in agony. He could not tolerate light, even the weak light thrown by a candle. He was seized by raging thirsts. Julep was prescribed to assuage the thirst, along with purges of senna and rhubarb with syrup of roses to wash his bowels. He was bled again and again. Cupping glasses were applied to draw off the humours and superfluous blood. A clyster was inserted into his bowel. Nothing helped.

When Charles first visited Henry's sickbed he found what one of the doctors told him was unicorn horn powder on the floor by Henry's bed. The powder had been poured in a circle and a spider put in it. When the spider died Henry's poison would be drawn, the doctor explained.

'What is all this hocus-pocus?' Charles blurted out to a groaning Henry.

Henry could hardly speak, but breathed out, 'Mayerne. Get Mayerne.'

A Calvinist, born in Geneva, Sir Théodore de Mayerne was one of London's leading doctors. He and Henry had had fascinating discussions about painting for years.

What intrigued Mayerne was not the art itself but the way substances, in this case colours, combined. What happens when a painter blends, say, green and blue? Or royal purple and red?

And it was not only colour which fascinated Mayerne. There was also thickness. A fifteenth century tempera painting is affected by the thick white gesso ground they used. How thick did the ground have to be to make it smooth to achieve a luminous tone to the work?

Henry, too, had become fascinated by these questions. Mayerne's assembly of papers on the subject, *Pictoria Sculptoria et quae subalternarum atrium*, discussed the properties of pigments, binders, mediums and varnishes. Henry had read it with interest.

Mayerne was blessed with an appearance which commanded respect and evoked reassurance, a huge asset in a physician. He had chubby hamster cheeks which could be puffed out to show judicious consideration, a distinguished looking white beard a third of the way down his chest to signal learning, and a straight Roman road of a nose to show decisiveness.

All these facial attributes were working away as Mayerne swilled Henry's urine around a large china chamber pot and examined and tasted the effluvia. It was whitish, watery and thin and tasted of salt.

Charles watched from Henry's bedside. Near the door, Elizabeth was weeping in Frederick's arms. Neither of Henry's parents had visited, though both were distraught.

'Well?' Charles said, sounding childish even to himself.

'He has the novum morbum,' pronounced Mayerne, nodding at the effluvia. 'Many are suffering its evil workings. Universal inflammation of the blood. It is occasioned by over violent exercise at tennis and overeating of grapes.'

After that, Mayerne, while appearing busily solicitous, took every opportunity to absent himself from Henry's bedside. He knew Henry would die within days. He knew the mass of physicians, summoned in growing desperation, would apply more and more superstitious remedies, so they could say at the end that everything had been tried.

Sure enough, Henry's head was shaved shortly afterwards. A live cockerel was applied to the soles of his feet and a dead pigeon tied to his head.

Sadly, to Charles, his many true friends, like William Cavendish, were forbidden his bedside, although the spirited and beautiful Frances Howard, Countess of Essex, came anyway, daring the physicians to try to stop her. Frances's kisses on his fevered forehead drew the last of Henry's smiles. She and Elizabeth wept in each other's arms.

Charles, Elizabeth and Frederick doubled and redoubled their visits. Charles played cards with Henry to amuse him for as long as he could stay awake. He had a Rubens picture at Oatlands, *Diana and her Nymphs Spied on by Satyrs*, brought into Henry's room to distract him.

The painting showed a devil figure drawing back the covering cloth of one of two women who were otherwise naked. The normally staid and prudish Charles even made a mildly ribald remark about the painting which succeeded in distracting Henry from his agony as much as anything on this earth could.

One of his majesty's chaplains, James Wilkinson, was summoned. He made the sign of the cross over Henry's enfeebled body and preached from Job XIV I: 'Man that is born of woman is of short continuance and full of trouble'. The same text was read at his funeral.

Henry knew he was going to die. His emaciated body was wracked by massive discharges of choler, phlegm and putrefied matter. When the time came, he managed to indicate with a wave of an emaciated arm that everybody should leave him except Charles. He gave Charles to understand that he wanted to ride. Charles naturally thought this an expression of his unhinged mind, but Henry had struggled back to reality for a final flourish of will.

'Get the horse,' he said, with immense difficulty. 'The Medici horse.'

Charles understood him. The small statuette of a bronze horse by Giovani Bologna was from the Medici collection, kept at Oatlands in Henry's Wunderkammer of small beauties. Charles fetched it and gave it to Henry. It was a graceful piece of power and movement, a pacing horse with rear-left and front-right legs off the ground, head down, prancing with joy at the wind in its mane.

'For you, bishop.' Henry rasped out the words painfully. 'Keep it. Remember me.'

Charles took the little statue, clutched it in his hand and watched until the rattling in Henry's chest subsided. He was eighteen years old. How could this be God's will?

Charles howled in visceral misery.

He did not believe such misery could ever be compounded. But it was: As the leading light of the nascent alliance between the small Protestant states, Frederick was offered the crown of Bohemia, to rule there as a Protestant ruler. The scattered Protestant kingdoms were all the keener on this plan as they assumed James would support his son-in-law, militarily if necessary, if any of the great Catholic powers – France, Spain or the Habsburg Empire – objected.

41

Frederick considered it his sacred duty to accept the throne of Bohemia, thus saving it from Catholic mysticism. Taking a thousand troops with him, he and Elizabeth rode to Prague where they were crowned king and queen of Bohemia. They promptly banished the religion of Rome from their kingdom.

A massive force of Catholic troops – mainly Spanish and Habsburg – then attacked Prague. Alarmed by a frantic note from his sister, Charles sent 2,000 livres from his private purse. Militarily, Charles and James did not have enough warning to help and lacked the troops anyway. The Bohemians fighting for Frederick allowed the attacking force to get between them and the city of Prague. They were cut off.

Elizabeth, who was pregnant, had insisted on staying with Frederick. She was at a separate camp though, away from the battle. Frederick went to visit her just as the Catholic force attacked. He missed the battle, which the Protestants resoundingly lost. He was branded a coward. He and Elizabeth had to flee the kingdom they had briefly ruled.

Worse was to follow. Charles, in agonies of worry for Elizabeth, received a message that the vengeful Catholic forces had continued the attack in Frederick's homeland. They drove him and Elizabeth out of their kingdom in the Palatinate, too. All their possessions were seized, including all their papers and the crown jewels.

The terrified couple escaped in a coach, bumping over bad tracks. Mounted Catholic forces would easily have overtaken them, were it not for a heroic rear-guard action by Frederick's household guard.

The homeless and penniless refugees headed for the Low Countries where they were given sanctuary by the Prince of Orange, the Stadholder, Frederick-Hendrik and his wife Amalia van Solms.

Elizabeth and Frederick had no kingdom, no money and no home. But they did have a baby, safely born, although such was the rush to escape he was thrown into the boot of a carriage by a nurse only at the last minute. They named him Rupert.

Charles wept at the thought of his sister and Frederick as penniless outcasts though at least they were safe. But how had it come to this? Charles remembered the days of hope, the staging of *The Hector of Germany* which he had seen with William Cavendish. By now old enough to visit the theatre alone, Charles took a carriage back to the Red Bull for a very different play.

*The Virgin Martyr* by Thomas Dekker, who had arranged the Lord Mayor's pageant, the last public event Henry ever attended, was about Elizabeth Stuart. Ironically borrowing heavily from Catholic saints' plays – tragedia sacra – the play lauded Elizabeth as a Protestant martyr. She is the invisible angel who comes down in Act IV to an accompaniment of wind music.

The Master of the Revels, Sir Henry Herbert, to Charles's fist-clenched fury, had objected to the play, apparently because he saw it as lauding Catholicism, the very opposite of the play's intention. Herbert had insisted on seeing the production script before publication and then, still apparently bewildered, after it.

Charles, with his new authority as heir to the throne, had icily explained the play to the Master of the Revels and it had then gone ahead. It was not a good play, in Charles's opinion, but it was about his darling sister.

Charles's utter misery at this time was alleviated to a degree by the first detailed letters from Elizabeth in The Hague. She and Frederick had arrived there by river from Delft, Elizabeth had written. They had a large townhouse on a boulevard known as the Voorhout paid for by the money Charles had kindly sent.

Charles stopped reading at that point. He remembered everything Elizabeth had done for him when they were children in Scotland. He said 'You are greatly welcome, darling sister' out loud. Then he cried.

# CHAPTER 5
## *THE MOST BEAUTIFUL MAN IN EUROPE*

George Villiers, Duke of Buckingham, was, by common consent, the most beautiful man in Europe. From the crown of his head to the sole of his foot there was no blemish upon him. Every motion, every bending of his body was admirable.

He had a mane of auburn hair flowing down to a wide ruff, a boldly moustachioed face, smooth-complexioned from daily washing in posset curd, above a body no Greek statuary-master could have improved.

Even those few dissenters who demurred from the most beautiful man in Europe designation acknowledged he had the best legs in Europe. Such legs – muscular but long, thin and graceful – could propel only a man who spent many hours in the saddle and who therefore lived the leisurely life of a courtier.

Buckingham had succeeded Robert Carr as James's 'favourite' – the object of his desires. James, who was prone to pet names, gave him the name Steenie, a diminutive form of Stephen. The name derived from Acts 6: 15: 'All who were sitting in the Sanhedrin looked intently at Stephen, and they saw that his face was like the face of an angel.'

Steenie's angelic looks had set his well-shaped feet on a road to great riches, many titles and a life of power and luxury if he complied uncomplainingly and submissively with everything James required of him. So far, his compliance had brought him the titles of Lord High Admiral of England, Lord Warden of the Cinque Ports, Constable of the Castle of Dover and of the royal Castle of Windsor, Lord President of the Council of War, Knight of the Garter and First Minister.

But, as Buckingham was unceasingly aware, the alternative to these accretions of glory, at the first flicker of disobedience or even reluctance, would be the Tower, probably for life. Steenie, though, was no Robert Carr, labile and prettily dim. He was highly intelligent, he was witty and he was a capable administrator, able to carry out any function of state well and with aplomb.

He was also physically brave and skilled in knightly valour – horse-riding, tilting the lance, sword fighting. He had won every prize at the tiltyard and was the only man in Europe held to be a better dancer than Raleigh. He could be haughty with people he did not know well, though warm and loyal once he counted you a friend. He had a flashing temper and he was a live-for-the-moment spendthrift, spending every penny that came his way on entertainment and rich living.

But not debauchery, never that. He was sustained by a tranquil, loving marriage to Katherine Manners, daughter of the Earl of Rutland, a great beauty and the richest heiress in England. Katherine adored him with a blind passion and worshipped him with the benison of her love.

His love for her ran less deep but he was fond of her, desired her strongly and enjoyed her company. The only problem with darling Katherine was that she had just converted to Catholicism, out of true belief. James was perturbed about that. And James perturbed meant trouble, perhaps disaster.

Buckingham had adapted well to the heady heights of court life from his relatively humble beginnings. He came from a family of minor gentry in Brooksby, Leicestershire. An important early move was to win over the young, immature Prince Charles who was eight years younger than him. But what had started as a tactical friendship was rapidly supplanted by genuine affection, then fondness, then love.

Like most people who got close to Charles, Buckingham liked him. And Charles hero-worshipped the urbane, dashing, witty man who was everything he could never be, just as Henry once was.

Charles even allowed Buckingham to use James's nickname for him, Baby Charles. He liked it from Buckingham, though he hated it from his father. Just as he had liked poor dead Henry calling him Bishop.

And as Henry had been, Buckingham was Charles's mentor in matters of art. Along with Arundel, he was one of the greatest and most knowledgeable virtuosi – collectors – of his time: He had corresponded with Rubens. Indeed, he had advised Charles to send a Rubens *Judith and Holofernes* back to the artist in Antwerp, because it was clearly the work of his pupils. Rubens, all courtly diplomacy, had apologised and produced a version with his own hand.

Buckingham had travelled to Italy. He knew the works of Italian painters like Jacopo Bassano, Tintoretto and Titian. He even possessed a copy of Titian's *Ecce Homo*. He knew the world, understood it, had mastered it. Buckingham could solve any problem, or so it seemed to Baby Charles.

So when Charles had an idea of how to help Elizabeth, who in her last letter had begged for his assistance in her plight, he brought the idea to Buckingham first. The idea frightened and excited Charles in equal measure, not least because it meant abandoning the Protestant alliance.

He would marry the Infanta Anna of Spain, thus allying England with the major Catholic power occupying Elizabeth's kingdom, in the hope of getting them to restore her as Queen of Bohemia and the Palatinate.

Charles would travel to Spain with Buckingham to arrange all this. There would be no advance warning; they would surprise the Spanish. He would be like St George rescuing a Protestant queen from the papist dragon – though by rather different means than St George had used. He would cut the Gordian knot of tangled diplomacy to save Elizabeth. That, at any rate, was the plan.

It was a madcap idea, certainly. It was an escapade, a lark. But Buckingham was keen on it. Any absence from James's depredations on his body was welcome, but especially now. He needed to let James, who forgot most things quickly these days, forget about Katherine's conversion. Also, a caper with Charles in foreign climes was welcome to Buckingham. It appealed to his sense of adventure.

Buckingham put the idea to James after he had been out all day hunting. They were in James's Privy Chamber at Whitehall. James wore a black silk doublet, thickly padded to protect him from assassination attempts by sword or dagger – he had survived three such attempts back in Scotland. He was also wearing huge trunk hose which made his skinny, slightly deformed, legs look even odder. He donned the thick-lensed glasses which he usually wore only for reading dispatches.

He looked ghastly, Buckingham thought, yellow in the face, hollow-cheeked, bleary-eyed, worn out. His health was failing. At fifty-seven he looked near the end.

As Buckingham had expected, James did not reject the plan out of hand. He mulled it over carefully. Buckingham had stressed that a marriage alliance with Spain was the only way to restore Elizabeth and Frederick to their own territory in the Palatinate and to recover Bohemia for them. No more of James's dreams of a military solution. These feeble attempts had failed, faced with the might of Spain, the largest army in Europe.

And another factor was in play which helped Buckingham's cause considerably: James had suddenly and capriciously released the suffering and landless Raleigh so he could resume the plundering of Spanish shipping he was so good at, as a privateer – a licensed pirate. Olivares, in panic at the damage Raleigh could do, had himself suggested a marriage between Charles and the Infanta Anna, if James would call Raleigh off.

Discussions had rumbled on for months. A fragile peace had been established with Spain, except for some of the wilder privateers. This had involved re-establishing an Embassy in Madrid. Buckingham had stayed there for a few weeks while negotiating trade with the Spanish, as had his Gentleman of the Chamber, Endymion Porter. Parliament had recently protested about this increasing closeness to Spain, provoking James to have the leading protester, a windbag called John Pym, arrested.

Olivares had promised Anna would bring 200,000 crowns as a dowry, a huge attraction for James. The exchequer would be transformed from its habitual bankruptcy to prosperity at a stroke. James would be free to carry on hunting every day, secure in his reputation as a peacemaker. A reputation which would not be too badly damaged by re-directing Raleigh and the other privateers to pillage the ships of Catholic France, once he was allied with Spain.

The time might be ripe for the marriage. Anna was six years younger than Charles. Despite his nickname, 'Baby Charles' was now twenty-three. After more cogitation, James said Buckingham and Charles could go. They were to travel to Spain incognito and arrange the marriage.

Baby Charles was in love. The Spanish king, Philip IV, had sent a painting of the Infanta Anna. Unbelievably, to Charles, they had neglected to say who the artist was. Charles remembered Frederick falling top-to-toe in love with his sister as soon as he saw her in the flesh. So it was with Charles and the Infanta Anna's portrait.

Was she not comely? She had thick tresses of fair hair. When he stared at her, hour after hour, a richly sensuous face met his adoring gaze. There were touches of both red and white in her complexion. She had large, languorous eyes, accentuated by arched eyebrows. She had full red lips. She had one of those noses where the point continues a long way past the nostrils. Dear little nose! Enchanting!

Charles dreamed of various futures with Anna. They would rule England wisely and well in bliss. They would stroll through fields hand-in-hand. He clearly saw them doing that. They would listen to lute music. They would have children, though Baby Charles was rather vague about the mechanisms of how that was to be achieved.

Charles Stuart was literally love-sick. He fell prey to the green sickness, a form of bloodlessness common to girls when they first menstruate. He was dizzy and kept fainting in front of the Infanta's picture.

The dash to Spain to marry the Infanta and save Elizabeth was top secret. Charles and Buckingham revelled in that. They chose pseudonyms; Charles was Jack Smith, Buckingham was Tom Smith.

'Impenetrable,' Buckingham said, straight-faced.

'Mmm well let's hope so,' said Baby Charles, who had taken him seriously.

Charles borrowed false beards from Inigo's stock of clothing for the masques. They tried them on at Whitehall and fell about laughing until they wept. They acted out impromptu scenes of Jack and Tom Smith passing unrecognised through immense dangers to rescue a fair damsel. This was rapidly extended to two fair damsels, Elizabeth and Anna, one aware of her need for rescue, the other, at present, unaware.

Charles felt happier than ever in his life before. He felt secure in Buckingham's protection, as if the older man had his arms round him all the time. He felt himself a loyal squire to Buckingham's knight-errant.

Endymion Porter, Buckingham's Gentleman of the Chamber, spoke Spanish like a native. He had read Cervantes's story about the moth-eaten knight, Don Quixote. He made sure his master had a copy of Thomas Shelton's translation, *The Delightful History of the Witty Knight Don Quixote*, as soon as it appeared.

Buckingham immediately adopted the role of Don Quixote. Charles was grateful enough to tag behind the handsome master as Sancho Panza.

Endymion Porter also explained the tradition of the 'generous unknown' in Spanish romance to Charles and Buckingham. The generous unknown gallantly places himself by the side of a cavalier engaged in unequal combat with many. He thrusts and he parries until some of the bravos are disabled and the rest put to flight.

Charles and Buckingham had been enthralled by this. Endymion was gently suggesting to his employer and his prince that they present themselves to the Spanish as the champions of the lone cavalier, Frederick, gallantly battling insuperable odds. The romance of it all delighted them.

# Chapter 6
## The Road to the Louvre

The long-anticipated day dawned; Charles and Buckingham set off. They had ridden as far as a small inn called The Leather Bottle not far from Maplesden, on the way to Dover. It had a grotesque portrait of James hanging over the fireplace, which the serving wenches overheard Charles criticising. They were pacified by the size of the lunch order: Fordwick trout, a chine of beef, plovers with white Gaillac wine and red Bordeaux.

A French gentleman stopped at their table and greeted them. It was the Comte de Tillières, the French ambassador.

'We are Jack and Tom Smith,' Buckingham said. 'How do you do?'

They had put the false beards on the table while they were eating. In any case, the ambassador knew them both well. He looked at Charles, especially, curiously. Charles wore his hair stiff with pomade. He sported a large starched ruff which pushed his head back. He had grown a pencil moustache in a failed attempt to look somewhere near his real age.

Charles and Buckingham hastily put their false beards back on and attempted to maintain the disguise. The Comte de Tillières, puzzled but mightily amused, said he was on his way to Dover and then France, as no doubt Prince Charles and the Duke of Buckingham were.

To the fascination of the innkeeper, the serving wenches and the other customers, Charles and Buckingham, holding their beards on, maintained their identities of Jack and Tom Smith. The Comte de Tillières listened politely then wished them a good journey. He said he hoped to see them again in Paris where his majesty King Louis XIII and Queen Anne of Austria would be honoured to receive them. And with a final courtly bow, sweeping his hat along the floor, the French ambassador was gone.

With characteristic humility, Endymion Porter was waiting for them outside Dover Castle. where Buckingham was warden. The whole of his huge figure appeared to smile. He looked like a benign mountain. Endymion was a devoted blood-and-bone royalist who was ready to engage the world for his master. He would truly have died to advance Buckingham's service and been proud to do it.

Endymion looked Spanish in his complexion and physiognomy, felt Spanish in his tastes, and in his blood was Spanish, or at least part Spanish. His maternal grandmother was a Spanish noblewoman, Dona Juana de Figueroa y Mont Salve. His English grandfather, Giles, married her when he lived in Spain, working as an interpreter.

As a boy, Endymion became a page in the service of Gaspar Olivares, the father of the Olivares currently dominating James's court. Nobody outside Spain knew the Spanish court as well as Endymion.

Charles stepped back to get Endymion in view, throwing his head back, which caused his broad brimmed hat to fall off. A gust took it and it blew along the ground. He retrieved it but lost his false beard in the process.

Meanwhile, Endymion enfolded Buckingham in a bear-like embrace into which Buckingham disappeared – Endymion being the only man Charles knew who was significantly bigger than Buckingham. Endymion then kissed him wetly on the cheek.

Faced with this familiarity, Charles remembered that Endymion was not only Buckingham's Gentleman of the Chamber and Master of Horse he was also his kinsman. Some four years ago he had married Olivia Boteler, Buckingham's niece. Like Buckingham's wife, Olivia was a Catholic, an advantage for the Spanish adventure, a massive handicap back in England.

Endymion bowed gravely to Charles, sweeping his hat along the ground in the Spanish and French manner. 'Your Highness.'

'Porter! What news of our venture?'

'Olivares has left the English court for Spain, Your Highness. I am sailing later today, but he will be there ahead of me. I have arranged your ship for early tomorrow but if you stop in Paris, as you intend, he will have been at the court for some time before you arrive.'

Buckingham roared. 'God's teeth! We've already met the French Ambassador. Anybody else got ahead of us on this surprise trip? How about the Pope, will he be there?'

Endymion smiled. 'No, my Lord!'

Buckingham was neither as angry nor a surprised as he pretended to be. Olivares's hold over James was so strong that James would have told him of the plan immediately. Endymion had been so circumspect with the news because he knew how deeply Buckingham loathed Olivares.

Men who delight women tend to dislike other men who delight women, and so it was with Buckingham and Olivares. Olivares had cut a swathe through the English court ladies, bedding all he desired. Buckingham, circumscribed in his true desires whenever James was present, was jealous.

Olivares gleefully fed this jealousy, waving out of his carriage window to passing females whenever he left his sumptuous dwelling in Ely Place in Holborn, passing from there to Drury Lane and the Strand, with quality ladies on balconies fluttering handkerchiefs and smiling as he passed.

Olivares was a small man, nothing like Buckingham's manly frame, but he had a knowingly powerful, handsome face with upturned moustaches.

'The Blockhead,' sighed Buckingham. It was his usual nickname for Olivares. 'We would have to deal with the Blockhead at some stage anyway. We might as well start as we mean to go on.'

'We met the French Ambassador by chance on the road,' Charles told Endymion. 'He guessed our intention to visit Paris and no doubt knows our final destination.'

Endymion gave a gentle smile. Charles had never known a man who exuded balm and goodwill as he did. 'No harm done,' he said, gently. 'But I must make haste. My ship sails soon.'

'Are you sailing on one of Tom's ships?' Buckingham said. Endymion's brother, Tom, was a sea captain.

'Indeed, yes, my Lord. I have arranged dinner for you at the Castle, in the Constable's Tower. I have told the lieutenant, Sir Harry Mainwaring, your tastes. You sail at dawn tomorrow on the *Anne Royal*. All other shipping from Dover has been stopped until you are clear. I will see you again in Madrid.'

'All well, Endymion,' said Buckingham. 'But is there news of Montagu? We need him, too. You cannot undertake the entire burden of translation alone.'

This was Wat Montagu, the Earl of Manchester's second son who was near perfect in Spanish.

'Ah. My privado.' He translated for Charles. 'My trusted confidant. We hope he will arrive soon. Your Highness, my Lord, I wish you a safe and enjoyable journey.'

And you, too, Endymion.'

'We thank you for this good service,' Charles said, awkwardly.

Endymion smiled.


Overnight at Dover Castle, Charles was in pain from the rickets in his joints. In his Spartan chamber, Buckingham lay him down tenderly on the trundle bed, tied his white linen nightcap on his head and treated him by candlelight, as he had often done before: First, a massage with soothing oils, then the application of a poultice of mallows and rye bran, boiled in wine and vinegar.

They sailed to France next morning on the *Anne Royal*, which reminded Charles not only of his mother but also of Henry, as the Master of the King's Ships, Phineas Pett, had presented it to Henry just after it was built. Although the *Anne Royal* coped sturdily with mountainous seas, Charles and Buckingham were copiously ill.

They were happily recovered by the time they reached Grande Rue in Boulogne, where they consumed a massive meal at the Ecu d'Or. They discussed, praised and drank to Endymion Porter, by now riding hard for Madrid.

They were delighted to be away, free, happy in each other's company, in France. Charles mentioned he was the first majesty to set foot on foreign soil since Henry VIII, who had notoriously been upended by the French king at the Field of the Cloth of Gold.

'Let's hope we have better luck with the Spanish,' Buckingham said. 'Not to mention the French on the way.'

After lunch, they crossed the bridge over the Liane and took the road to Montreuil. Buckingham had challenged Charles to a wager over which of them fell off the horse's back the least. So far Buckingham was winning, though not by as much as might have been expected. Under the Riding Master, M de St Antoine's, expert instruction Charles had become a competent horseman – his thighs were quite well developed, perhaps in compensation for deficiencies elsewhere.

They skirted the forest of Crecy, where Edward III won his famous battles. Charles wondered if his reign, when it came, would bring glory on England. He hoped so. Yet again, he pictured his future bride, the Infanta and their coming wonders together.

At Amiens, they attended evening mass. Charles was in excelsis at the beauty of the service and at the Gothic cathedral. Could he accept becoming a Catholic for the wonder of it? He knew the Spanish would wish it, but it would have to be done discretely, probably secretly. Meanwhile, perhaps the Anglican church could gradually adopt some elements of the Catholic mass. Charles mused dreamily on the idea.

They reached Paris as dusk was darkening the streets, entering by the Porte Saint Denis, which Buckingham told him was one of the older portals built by Charles IX. Buckingham seemed to know his way around the elegant French capital and to understand the argot shouted in the streets.

When Charles asked him, he explained that he had lived in Paris for three years, starting in his late teens. He said his father did not know what to do with him and shipped him off. He said he had learned riding in France – manège, how to ride big tournament horses. But above all he had learned to dance and cut capers; the dancing he was master of and famous for.

They reached a post house at the sign of the Grand Cerf in the Rue St Jacques where they took two basic but comfortable rooms for the night. Within minutes, there was a polite knock on the door. Louis's court tailor, M Marolles, appeared. He had been alerted by the French ambassador, who had had them followed since they entered Paris. M Marolles had come to measure them for two suits to wear at the French court at the Louvre. So much for the trip being clandestine, thought Charles.

M Marolles had brought the suits with him and needed only to alter them. Charles was resplendent in a white velvet doublet and hose flashed with azure silk and a cloak lined with the same material. Buckingham had a red slashed velvet doublet, red hose and a red cloak trimmed with fur. As often when he was especially gorgeously attired he thought back to the rustic threadbare black suit he had arrived in at court with only £50 a year to his name.

In those days, he was constantly crossing his legs to hide the holes in his hose.

Then another knock at the door. A certain M. Gaston also appeared, the court perruquier, who offered a choice of periwigs a la mode de la cour. These offered some disguise to the features, as Charles and Buckingham were still maintaining the Jack and Tom Smith identities, still revelling in the absurd transparency of the escapade.

A carriage drove them to the Louvre Palace. As they passed Les Halles market, Buckingham pointed out to Charles the exact spot, in the Rue de la Ferronnerie, where Henri IV of France had been stabbed to death by an assassin in his coach.

The Louvre Palace presented a wall of windows which reminded Charles of the Cavendish place, Hardwick Hall. He thought fondly of William Cavendish, who had taken him to see Wentworth Smith's play *The Hector of Germany* all those years ago when the world looked so full of promise.

As their carriage came to a halt, Charles snorted at the Louvre Palace. He and Inigo would do better than all this flat glass, one day they would. Oh, most certainly! Inspired by Palladio, they would dream up the most superb palace in Europe. This place would look like a bothy in comparison.

They were welcomed on the gravel drive by a smiling French ambassador, the Comte de Tillières who asked them if they had had a good journey here since he had last seen them at the Leather Bottle inn. Buckingham glared at him.

De Tillières then asked if they wished him to present them to His Majesty King Louis XIII and Queen Anne of Austria. Anne of Austria, as Charles well knew, was his beloved Infanta's older sister, as well as sister to the King of Spain, who they were on their way to meet. He opened his mouth to accept the invitation. It was still open when Buckingham courteously refused it.

The Comte de Tillières bowed his acceptance of the rebuff. He smoothly said (in English) that there would be a masque for their entertainment soon, in the Pavilion des Arts, followed by dancing in the Pavilion de Beauvais. He then glided away.

Charles and Buckingham followed the elegant crowd to the Pavilion des Arts. As in Whitehall, the seats were on three sides of the stage. Charles and Buckingham sat in the front row, on the left-hand side.

Louis was at the front on a throne-like chair facing the middle of the stage. Charles twisted in his seat in an undignified manoeuvre to look at him. He had black curly hair and a pursed mouth below an extravagant moustache, waxed upwards. He was slight and unprepossessing, almost buried by a damask crimson mantle embroidered with gold and precious stones. Charles had heard that he, too, stuttered, though by all accounts not as badly as Charles himself.

There was no sign of his queen. Either she was not attending or, as her namesake, his mother Anne had once done, she was taking the chance to express herself in the freedom of dance, in the masque. In that case she would appear soon.

Directly behind Louis, at the back of the theatre, on a throne of a chair as large as the King's sat a moustachioed figure with a beard known as an imperial. He was draped in a Cardinal's red robes, topped with a red skull-cap. Puffed pride seemed to billow his robes below the lean, ruthless face. Even at this distance, through the throng, Charles could feel his black eyes in his back.

So this was Armand Jean du Plessis, the fabled Cardinal Richelieu, known as the red eminence. He was the most powerful man in France, quite possibly in Europe. To Charles's amazement the guards around him, armed with long swords in leather baldrics, wore a rich red, like the Cardinal, not green as Louis's men were liveried. Richelieu evidently had his own private army.

Charles glanced hastily away, up at the coffered ceiling, round at the wood panelling with balconies. Not bad. The audience in their Parisian finery, appeared happy enough. The masque to be performed, it was announced, was a traditional piece called the *Ballet Comique de la*

*Reine.* The music started. The noise of chatter, if anything, increased.

There was no printed summary of the masque, as was usual at Whitehall, but Charles and Buckingham both knew the *Ballet Comique de la Reine.* It was a traditional piece dating back to the heady days of Gloriana in England and Henry III in France. It centred on the story of the enchantress Circe, from Homer's Odyssey.

Charles noticed with smug satisfaction that the evolution of the scenes was achieved by footmen dismantling and then erecting scenery in front of which the dancers danced. Inigo's ingenious machines, as they had even at country houses in England, were clearly unknown here.

Charles was about to remark on this to his companion, when he noticed a vast and strange transformation in Buckingham. His face was set rigid in a mask, eyes staring. At first Charles thought dear George was thinking of James's depredations on his body, which also set his face in an other-worldly mask. But this frozen face was one of transport.

Circe had arrived on the stage on a tiered fountain, surrounded by lady dryads. She was played by the queen, Anne of Austria, who was indeed beautiful. Charles hoped her sister, his own beloved Infanta of Spain, would prove to be of equal beauty.

Did that account for the transformation in Buckingham? Evidently it did. He was staring fixedly at her, his mouth slightly open. People around them were already beginning to stare, some tittering, the ladies fluttering their fans like alarmed birds about to take off.

Meanwhile, on the stage, Tempe, the classical valley in Thessaly between Mount Olympus and Mount Ossa, has been haunted by the enchantments of Circe and her beasts. It was being restored to its original beauty as the home of the muses. This transformation took place in front of them while the beauteous Anne of Austria, as the enchantress Circe, cavorted.

Buckingham started to talk to himself. Charles looked at him, alarmed. He was describing her scanty clothes in a near deranged manner: 'A garment of watchet satin, with stars of silver, embroidered and embossed from the ground. And on her head a crown of stars, mixed with some falls of white feather.'

The Queen appeared to smile at Buckingham, certainly to notice the concentrated focus of his total attention, the prisms of his eyes shining a burning light from within.

Charles was momentarily distracted by one of Circe's attendant dryads. She was a tiny, skinny girl, surely no more than thirteen, with scrawny arms and shoulders, in a diaphanous green-blue dress and high cork-soled shoes which she extravagantly kicked off and left in a heap.

This girl broke from the group of her companions to dance barefoot sinuously in front of Charles and Buckingham, flashing a toothy grin. To Charles's great surprise, her performance was clearly aimed at him, not at Buckingham.

The second the masque was over, after an hour or so, Buckingham imperiously waved to the French ambassador, de Tillières, who made his way through the throng to join them.

'Will the Queen be at the dancing at the Pavilion des Arts, which is now to follow?' Buckingham's tone made the words coarse. If anything it sounded even ruder in French, which they were now speaking.

De Tillières gave a practised diplomatic smile. 'I believe so, Your Excellency. Would your Excellency like me to present you to His Highness and Her Majesty after all? My King is most anxious to…'

'That will not be necessary. Lead us to the Pavilion de Beauvais, if you please.'

On the way out, tamely following the French ambassador, Charles glimpsed the Cardinal, still enthroned at the focal point of the room. His face was thunderous.

At the Pavilion de Beauvais the orchestra was already playing. Buckingham stared at the door until Louis and Anne appeared. She had changed into a yellow satin basquina with a frothy lace bodice which showed her perfect curves to advantage. Her lips were newly reddened, her cheeks were pink. She was clutching a cambric handkerchief in her left hand, looking confidently ahead with amused curiosity.

Next to her, Louis twirled his moustache and placed one hand on his hip. Buckingham sneered at him. He was a fool. As Buckingham recalled, he was known to talk little except to his dogs in a language he had invented. Woof, woof.

More to the point, he wished to be known as Louis the Chaste, after the proud non-consummation of his marriage when he and Anne were both fourteen. Shortly afterwards, he had her Spanish Ladies in Waiting sent away and replaced by French women who forced her to dress and behave in the French manner, leaving her feeling isolated and miserable. This was a matter of indifference to Louis. He had absolutely no interest in her, as a person or as a woman.

In stark contrast, Buckingham's fixed, concentrated, utter absorption with Anne was continuing to attract attention. The orchestra struck up a galliard, dating back to the period of the masque they had just seen. Buckingham strode over to Louis and Anne, ignored the King completely, seized Anne by the hand and led her into the dancing.

As Charles watched, one of many pairs of eyes, Buckingham performed the cadence jumps to the music in front of the queen. He was like a diabolic dervish in red, auburn hair flowing, landing with one leg ahead of the other in perfect posture. The queen blushed, smiling slightly, then squealed as he seized her round the waist in the close hold of the lavolta.

While she was pinioned against him in the air, in front of the court and gentry of France, Buckingham breathed into her ear.

'Madam, is there a closed chamber, or an anteroom near here? I must ravish you. Here. Now. Or I die.'

Anne was crushed against him. She smiled. 'Best lower me to the floor, sir, while you compose yourself.'

He swung her round, still three feet off the ground. 'Damn composure. Damn lowering. Damn anything that isn't you. Come madam, am I to live or die? Embrace me while I ravish you or call your guards. Which is to be?'

Anne dropped her cambric handkerchief on the floor. For a moment, the beats of the galliard sounded loudly in a silence between them.

'You are travelling to the Spanish court tomorrow, sir,' she said, in her heavily accented French. 'Aren't you, Bourkinkam. George?'

'Yes. What of it?'

'The lavolta is finished. For God's sake put me down.' He did so. The dancing went on around them. 'I had a presentiment you would die for me. I saw you in a dream, stabbed and bleeding.'

'I had the same presentiment. What does it mean?'

'If you die in France I could not forgive myself.'

She said something in Spanish.

'Tell me what you just said, Anne or I swear to God I will ravish you here as we stand and the guards can kill me when I have finished.'

'I said I will meet you if you wish to converse with me. But slowly, Bourkinkam Slowly.'

'Alright. And give me a keepsake of you. I need something with me always.'

She nodded, seeing an excuse to escape to catch her breath. 'Alright. I will fetch something from my chamber and meet you by the door. Do not try to follow me, Bourkinkam.'

'I possess you or I die, Anne. There never was a more solemn vow.'

Her eyes were wide. 'Vous serez servi au point nommé, Bour-kin-kam.' You shall be served in any way you please.

Then she was gone. When she returned, he met her at the great oak double doors of the Pavilion de Beauvais.

'Here,' she said. 'A keepsake, as you want of me.'

The keepsake was an exquisite rosewood casket with her monogram carved on it in gold. Buckingham took it, fell on his knees in front of her and kissed the hem of her dress.

His Eminence, the Cardinal Richelieu, had made his way to the Pavilion de Beauvais, surrounded by men of his faction and his guards. All Richelieu had known of Buckingham before this evening was that he had become one of the leading art collectors in Europe, and he was on intimate terms with Rubens. Rubens was an agent of Spain as well as a painter.

The cardinal resented English entry into the art market, driving up prices and taking paintings his Eminence wanted for himself. Buckingham, in particular, had a reputation for paying over the odds. He became frantic when he wanted something and would stop at nothing to get it. But the cardinal's resentment at all that was as nothing to his seething fury at this evening's humiliation of the French monarchy and court at the hands of this low-born English upstart.

Charles had been glancing at Richelieu, as well as watching with alarm as Buckingham made his intentions clear to the entire French court. The cardinal's face was black as he muttered instructions to one of his cronies, the Count of Soubise. They were nodding at Buckingham and Anne.

Charles feared for Buckingham's life.

# CHAPTER 8
## THE SWORN ENEMY

Early next morning, Charles and Buckingham left Paris by the La Villette gate. Buckingham had not wanted to leave at all. Over breakfast, he had refused to ride away from Anne, whose image consumed him. It was only the wild hope that her brother, Philip, King of Spain, or her sister, the Infanta, would advance his cause in some mysterious way that persuaded him to saddle up the horses at all.

For a while, he rode furiously in bitter silence as the sun rose. Then, riding slightly ahead of Charles, who could see only his back, Buckingham poured forth a torrent of words into the air. To Charles's amazement, the subject of this gushing out of pain was not Anne of Austria but James.

'The sin of sodomy is worthy of condign punishment,' Buckingham said, in one breath.

'George, are you alright?'

'You don't go hunting with him, do you? He is a monster who creates monsters out of those he corrupts. He created the Steenie monster with deeds and with that revolting baby-talk.'

'I know.'

Buckingham stroked the mane of his piebald horse as he pressed it forward. 'At the hunt, he is so fat he can hardly ride without grooms holding the reins. When we have followed a deer for miles he will personally slit its throat and feed the entrails to the dogs. Then he has me held fast and stripped naked. The attendants daub me with the blood of the deer while the dogs are held near me on leashes, driven wild with the blood. He then smears the blood all over my body with his palms flat, while the dogs are brought even nearer. When I am in sufficient state of terror, he attempts sodomy while the grooms and courtiers are made to watch. He whispers in my ear: "My own sweet dear little child." If he is unable to fulfil his desires on me, on occasion he lets the grooms do his business for him.'

Buckingham slowed the horse, then tumbled acrobatically out of the saddle while holding onto the reins, finally pulling the horse up. He tied the horse to a bush, knelt on the grass and retched until he vomited back his breakfast.

Charles, too, felt himself starting to heave. Against his will, he recalled the masque at Theobalds, which resounded in the folklore of James's court. He had been a child then, what, six years old? As ever, the masque should have been a thing of beauty. Inigo had painted the backdrops, Ben Jonson had conjured the words. As part of a four-day feast, the personifications of Law Justice and Peace welcomed the visiting guest of honour from over the seas.

Charles spoke out loud. 'It should have been a thing of beauty.' But it was not. James had unleashed one of the most hideous of his debaucheries on the audience. The masque at Theobalds, bestial and depraved even by James's standards, had destroyed his mother because the visiting guest of honour from over the seas was her brother, the unsuspecting Christian IV, King of Denmark.

Afterwards, Charles's mother had sunk into grey melancholy. She became a Catholic to find a refuge and spite her husband, but it was not enough.

After that, Buckingham set a furious pace to the Spanish frontier, which they crossed at a narrow pass in the Pyrenees. After France, the poverty of Spain was stark. The countryside was bare, the peasants tilling it in rags. There were hardly any inns and where there were they had no beds and no food. They bought bread and milk at farmhouses. They rode hard, covering nearly sixty miles a day, arriving in Madrid in the first week of March, in the middle of Lent.

As they passed through the gates, Charles saw two gorgeously attired bravos. He noticed their hats first; wide, upturned brims, high crowns and a resplendent plume of a feather, ready to be gallantly swept along the floor. Their wild love locks flowed out from their hats, round elegant waxed moustaches and down to chin beards.

One of the laughing bucks had pale blue plumage, the other green. They had elaborate shoulder-belts for their swords into which they had tucked rich, tan gauntlet gloves. Their legs showed to advantage in yellow and scarlet Spanish hose, with false calves, and spur-leathers.

All in all they were a perfect courtly blend of elegance and power, chivalry and might. Buckingham caught Charles's open-mouthed wonder at them, his fixed gaze. 'Caballeros,' he said with a smile.

'Which you would translate as... as...'

'Cavaliers.'

The Embassy was a building of Moorish design in the Calle de las Infantas. Inside, there was an air of hubbub, if not panic, with people dashing hither and yon. From his previous stay at the Embassy, when it was first established, Buckingham recognised the broad frame of Henry Jermyn and the Earl of Manchester's oldest son, Edward. He was looking for Edward's younger brother, Wat Montagu, but there was no sign of him.

Endymion Porter peeled away from the throng to welcome the travellers with a low bow.

'Greetings, Your Majesty, Your Excellency.' And then, as if reading Buckingham's mind, 'Wat Montagu was delayed at Dover, my Lord. But he will be arriving soon.'

'Good,' boomed Buckingham. He gave a windy sigh of mixed exhaustion and relief. 'I want us to use our own translators at all times, Endymion. Olivares is capable of any kind of legerdemain and deception.'

Endymion smiled. 'Of course, my Lord. What news of home?'

Endymion was looking anxious.

'Olive is well, Endymion,' Buckingham said, clapping the giant hard on the forearm. 'She and your boy, young Charles, send their love. How old is Charles now?'

'Three, my Lord.'

'Good, good. All are well. My Kate is well. We will be back in their soft bosoms soon enough, bearing our triumph.'

Endymion grinned broadly at that. Charles gave a smile. All activity at the Embassy had now stopped. Everybody was listening to Buckingham.

The ambassador, John Digby, Earl of Bristol, had been standing behind Endymion for some time. He cleared his throat, furious at being ignored. Buckingham had clashed with him frequently in the past, the worst time being Buckingham's last stay at the Embassy. The two grandees loathed one another.

'You got a cough, Digby?' enquired Buckingham, pretending to notice him for the first time. 'Too much time in the heat.'

Digby favoured that with a sardonic smile, even the pretence of a cordial greeting gone. The ambassador had been working assiduously toward a trade agreement with the Spanish. These manoeuvrings for a marriage alliance had completely scuppered his talks, talks which had been going on for nearly a year now. A year's work gone up in flames, as Digby saw it.

John Digby was forty-three, of medium height and had grey eyes set in an undistinguished face. He had an upturned, waxed Spanish moustache, a stiffly starched standing ruff which appeared to bristle when Buckingham goaded him, and an expression of concentrated, cold arrogance.

He saw Buckingham as impetuous to the point of rashness, arrogantly frivolous and self-glorifying. He made no secret of being a sworn enemy of the 'upstart favourite'. His quip that Buckingham had James's ear and James had Buckingham's arse had been repeated to Buckingham many times.

'Digby, a word. Anteroom. Now. Can't wait.'

John Digby's face tightened but he led the way to the anteroom of his office. Charles followed like a spaniel, because he always followed Buckingham. It was the first time he had seen his beloved George in action on business. It was terrifying.

'Sit down, Digby.'

'You arrogant bastard, Villiers.'

'Very well, stand up. I have written instructions from His Majesty putting me in sole charge of the negotiations over the marriage alliance. You are to stay away from the negotiations. Understood? I take it our rooms are prepared?'

'Charming as ever, Buckingham. Your wit is fabled. But to the matter at hand: Yes, accommodation is ready for you here for one night but from tomorrow the Spanish have arranged suites for his Highness and for you at the Escorial. Philip will meet you tomorrow. Olivares will conduct the negotiations from their side.'

'I thought he might.'

'Yes. He's the one you have to worry about, not Philip. He hates your guts of course. I can't think why.'

Buckingham gave a grim smile at that.

'How long do you think this will take, Buckingham? We have other matters in hand, at the Embassy, you know.'

Buckingham shrugged. 'Couple of weeks.'

'Hmm. Chalk is not scissors, my dear George.'

Charles glanced questioningly at Buckingham. For a moment, he did not understand the proverb, but then remembered it meant a tailor may chalk out a plan but it is nothing until he has scissors to cut it out. Charles thought the proverb rather apposite for the moment. Buckingham evidently did not.

'Isn't there a proverb, Digby to the effect that only asses and washerwomen quote proverbs? I may be wrong.'

'You usually are.'

'And what are the auguries like?' This was another jibe, Digby was known to be superstitious and had frequently consulted astrologers.

'The auguries, Villiers, are terrible. The Spanish expect His Highness to convert to Catholicism. Here. Now. They can't imagine why else he has come. Without that there will be no marriage agreement from their side. They will also want any children of His Highness and the Infanta to be raised as Catholics.'

'Oh dear,' said Charles. 'I don't... don't... don't...'

Digby droned on in a flat monotone. 'They will also want guarantees for recusants in England. Of a firmness that would have London ablaze in riot.'

'Well, you know what they say about Spain, Digby. Don't eat the fruit and don't mention religion.'

'The fruit is of the forbidden sort, you cocksure cockscomb. And before you ask, the chance of an armed intervention by Spain against its own Catholic allies in the Palatinate or Bohemia are zero. You can forget any aid for Frederick and Elizabeth.'

'I wasn't going to ask, as it happens. Diplomatic intervention?'

'A very slight chance. You would have to be half in bed with France and/or ready to unleash the privateers.'

This was genuinely useful but Buckingham masked his gratitude. 'I see.'

'I doubt you do. And Villiers, one more thing. They will almost certainly involve the Pope if only to delay the issue even further.'

'Heard from him, have you? The Holy Father?'

This was a dig at John Digby's kinsman, Everard Digby, who had been involved in the Catholic plot against James, two years into his reign. They had tried to blow up Parliament.

John Digby ignored the provocation. 'The Spanish will play for time, Villiers. That is what they do. That is how they think. Now that you have landed here like a mouse in a trap they can keep you here forever if they wish to. Drake and Raleigh can't reach you here. That is how they view the matter.'

'Very interesting, Digby, but I was weary before you started and as ever your discourse has increased my weariness. I take it there are letters awaiting us, no doubt one at least from England, from His Majesty?'

Digby ignored Buckingham and addressed his reply to Charles. 'Your Highness, all the correspondence to date arrived for you is on the desk in your rooms. If you have any wish at all during your unfortunately all-too-brief stay at the Embassy, please do let me know.'

Charles nodded earnestly. 'Thank you, Digby. I shall tell my father how helpful and welcoming you have been.'

Digby bowed from the waist. 'Thank you, Your Highness.'

As he and Charles walked out, Buckingham muttered, 'Always up somebody's arsehole, aren't you, Digby.'

'I learned from the best, Villiers.'

Buckingham muttered to himself. 'And now I suppose we had better read the old bastard's letter so we can reply to it and get some sleep.'

Charles and Buckingham had arrived at the Embassy in the late afternoon. By the time they went up to their suite of rooms it was early evening and candles had been lit. But the travellers could still just make out the snow covered Guadarrama mountains in the distance out of the window. They could hear bells from the nearby convent of

San Francisco. They were foreign bells, higher and more plangent than those at home.

In Charles's suite of rooms on the second floor he and Buckingham glanced at the pile of letters. Buckingham sat in an armchair and sorted letters to the top, from James, from his wife, Katherine and from Elizabeth in The Hague.

He gave the letter from James to Charles and read his letter from Kate:

My darling George,

You are a jewel that will win the hearts of all the women in the world, but I am confident it is not in their power to win your heart from a heart that is was and ever shall be yours till death. Everybody tells me how happy I am in my husband and how chaste you are, that you will not look at another woman and yet know they woo you.

Your loving and devoted Kate

Buckingham finished the letter with tears of misery in his eyes. Charles did not notice. He was at the desk the ambassador had provided, reading the letter from Elizabeth. It was very different from the despairing pleas for help she had sent in the past.

Addressing Charles as 'dearest of brothers', Elizabeth wrote at length about her life with Frederick in The Hague.

They lived in the court district, the Binnenhof, an area where elegant houses and promenades formed the centre of society life. There were fashionable shops where the beau monde disported themselves.

Their house was in Kneuterdijk, in the spacious former residence of Johan van Oldenbarnevelt, a leading Dutch statesman and fighter for Dutch freedom against Spain. They had also just bought the property next door, the

Wassenaer Hof, an elegant building in its own grounds which they were now furnishing richly.

They were enjoying the local hunting. She reminisced about boar hunting at Christmas and said the hare hunting season was just starting.

Towards the end of her letter, she said, with a sense of some excitement, that she and Frederick were being supported by the Merchant Adventurers. This was an English trading company based in Delft, very near The Hague. They had just thrown a celebration for her and Frederick at the Prinsenhof in Delft. They had loaned her a considerable sum of money, although she could always do with more to renovate and furnish their properties.

To illustrate their lives, Elizabeth had sent an engraving by Adriaen van de Venne showing a family in an elegant carriage pulled by prancing horses past gracious trees, with a graceful step-gabled house in the background.

Furthermore, Elizabeth wrote, the authorities in The Hague had welcomed the royal couple fulsomely. They had taken them to Amsterdam to see a play by the famous Dutch playwright Joost van den Vondel called *Jerusalem Destroyed*. The seizing of Jerusalem by Titus in 70AD was shown as a parable of Elizabeth and Frederick's loss of their capital, Heidelberg, and the Palatinate. By this means the authorities had shown their sympathy for the royal martyrs of the Protestant cause.

Charles wordlessly handed the letter to Buckingham, who sighed. 'This does not aid our mission, does it?'

'What do you mean?'

'What I mean, Baby Charles, is that the more settled and prosperous Elizabeth and Frederick are in their new life, the less urgency or even justification there is to rescue them from it. Would they even thank us? They are living in Oldenbarnevelt's old house as we betray the Protestant cause.'

'Are we betraying the Protestant cause?'

'We're having a damn good try, Baby Charles, because there is more money to be had from Spain. Beati Pacifici, you see, Baby Charles. That is us.'

Buckingham quoted James's motto, Blessed are the Peacemakers, with bitter irony.

# CHAPTER 9
## AT THE ESCORIAL

Before he left London, Charles had spent happy hours with Inigo Jones in the library at Whitehall, while the Surveyor of the King's Works explained the Escorial Palace to his willing royal pupil. Inigo began by unfolding a ground plan on the massive oak table where Charles and Henry had once been taught drawing by their tutor, Henry Peacham.

Silently and with perfect concentration, Inigo drew a flawless circle freehand round the edges of the plan, so the circle touched the angle of each corner of the square of the plan. It was a conscious imitation of Giotto, demonstrating his expertise at limning by drawing a perfect circle freehand.

Charles started to speak, or rather to babble, but Inigo sternly waved him to silence. Inigo had not yet finished. His mouth set with concentration, he then drew a triangle freehand inside the circle. The effect on Charles was one of magical symbols whose meaning was beyond reason.

'Vetruvius,' he murmured.

Inigo nodded solemnly. 'Yes. This shows the ideas of proportion of the great architect Vetruvius. They are ideas I put into practice with my design for the new Banqueting House.'

'But, but, but... The circle and the triangle. What does it mean?'

'What it means, Your Highness, is less important than the fact that it has a meaning at all.'

'Meaning?'

'The architect of the Escorial was Juan de Herrera. His ideas were influenced by a philosopher, a Catalan called Raymond Lull. Then later he was influenced by the treatises of Giovanni Paolo Lomazzo. They have been translated into English by Richard Haydocke if you want to read them. They deal with the magical interpretation of art.'

Charles nodded vigorously. 'Yes. I thought there was something ma… ma… magical about the circle and the triangle.'

'There is. Lomazzo believes in the artist realizing an idea, a single idea, from his mind into stone. That is the magic. In the Escorial, the Spanish King Philip II, who it was built for, is identified with Solomon. So the Escorial was deliberately built as a re-creation, not an imitation, a re-creation, of the Temple of Solomon. Solomon and his world, his art and his ideas, live on in the Escorial. That is the magic.'

The King, Philip IV, had sent a caroche for them, a more luxurious carriage than Charles had in London. It had the Spanish royal crest emblazoned on the doors. Charles was sitting next to Buckingham. Endymion Porter was sitting opposite as the carriage jolted along…

They had been travelling for over an hour. Charles's and Buckingham's luggage was in a wagon travelling behind.

Suddenly, in a blaze of sunshine, they emerged from forest to the heights overlooking the valley of the River Manzanares, now a feeble trickle in the glowering heat. And there it was.

Even after Inigo's elevated descriptions, Charles was not disappointed. The Escorial was a Moorish palace, built of granite hewn from the neighbouring sierra. Endymion explained that it was a palace, a church, a convent and a royal mausoleum all in one. There were three kings in the Podridero, or royal vault, Charles V, Philip II and Philip III.

The concept offered a scale and also a continuity Charles could only envy. His father, after all, was the first Stuart ruler and a small, twisted successor awaited when he died. It was all very shaky, this Stuart rule from the rickety palace at Whitehall.

But here was this vast and magnificent pile, embracing the past, defying the future. Peacocks from the menagerie wandered the front courtyard, splashing colour. They entered by two Moorish gates into a spacious court studded with cupolas and minarets. Above those, an ancient keep towered, with zig-zag battlements and turrets at each angle. Charles lost himself in a reverie of King Solomon once dwelling in such a temple.

Inside, there was a massive marbled hall, an airy place of quiet and stillness. Back at Whitehall, people scurried about, backwards and forwards, moving and pushing and tut-tutting. The atmosphere was as much marketplace as palace. The interior was so dilapidated visitors expected pieces to fall off as they walked past. This sometimes happened.

But here there was nobody about except an army of lackeys in a bewildering array of liveries. Endymion decoded some of their varying uniforms to an open-mouthed Charles: Just by their uniforms he pointed out grooms of the stable, arquebusiers, alabraderos and footmen holding blazing torches, even in broad daylight.

Until now, the most footmen Charles had ever seen in one place had been those hired for Elizabeth's wedding to Frederick. The bill for the liveries alone had nearly emptied the permanently shallow Stuart coffers. But here there were many-hued footmen everywhere, thick as flies, but moving more like circling bees.

And when passers-by did appear, with that languid gait they all had, they were dressed in silken doublets of various hues, velvet cloaks richly embroidered and plumed and jewelled hats. They were strolling splendour to Charles's wide-eyed gaze. There were no women to be seen. By now Charles had forgotten the Infanta altogether.

With Buckingham growing impatient, indeed beginning to curse like a Thames waterman, Endymion finally managed to locate a seneschal who gave his name as Don Fennyn. This notable bade them wait and fetched Olivares.

The handsome former ambassador greeted Charles and Endymion warmly, managing to snub Buckingham by giving him a cursory nod with a frozen thin smile. He had them ushered them to an anteroom off the main hall, explaining, without apology, that His Majesty was out hunting.

'But may I offer you refreshment? Some sack? Some wine? A few sweetmeats perhaps?'

Buckingham curtly refused sustenance, though Charles would have accepted.

The seneschal, Don Fennyn, arranged for their baggage to be transferred to two suites on the first floor of the Escorial. They were allocated one hundred servants and given a golden key which would open any lock in the palace, including, Olivares informed them, the lock to the royal bedchamber.

'Ah, and I have a surprise for you,' Olivares continued, smoothly. 'Wait one moment, please.'

Olivares disappeared, gliding away in that unhurried but smooth way they all had, as if they rolled along on small wheels. The surprise turned out to be the bounding entrance of Wat Montagu, loping in almost at a run.

'Wat!' Buckingham looked happy for the first time since they had left France. Wat Montagu, like Endymion, was in his employ, part of his household. He ruffled the young man's thick chestnut hair familiarly but with great affection.

'Your Excellency. Your Highness.' Wat Montagu bowed stiffly from the waist, as his doublet was sewn to his hose nothing more servile was possible. 'Hello Endymion!'

Wat Montagu and Endymion Porter hugged one another. This involved Montagu disappearing temporarily altogether. Endymion was a Goliath in any case but his bulk was emphasised by 'little Wat Montagu' as he was often known. His smiling, boyish features were lively and regular and his small form well-made. Charles liked him on sight.

He knew he was Sir Henry Montagu, the Earl of Manchester's younger son, but had never met him. Sir Henry was known as something of a tyrant but even so, Charles thought James had treated him shabbily.

Sir Henry had paid James £20,000 for the post of Lord Treasurer but then had to give it up ten months later, because James had found a favourite he wanted to give it to. Sir Henry had been summarily demoted to President of the Council.

'Where did you spring from, Wat?' a newly animated Buckingham boomed. 'It is good to see someone actually alive in this bloody mausoleum. You are alive aren't you, Wat? I've not been touched by Lethe's hand and woken in the middle of *A Midsummer Night's Dream* or something?'

Wat Montagu grinned his attractive urchin grin, all shapely mouth below a strong nose. 'No, my Lord. I am all too real and at your service. I was in the library, reading up on some theology.'

'You m-m-must tell me about it, Wat,' Charles said, anxious to get a word in and not be overlooked.

'I would be delighted to, Your Highness. I believe, if it please Your Highness, my Lord Buckingham wishes me to act as your guide and interpreter in the art markets they have in Madrid and on other pleasurable occasions, also perhaps with the Infanta, while Endymion is engaged in translating for the negotiations.'

'Excellent!' Charles said.

Wat Montagu, it later transpired, was just four years younger than he was. It occurred to Charles that he had never had a friend of his own age. He had had distant guiding stars, first Henry now Buckingham. He had had loving guardianship and protection from Elizabeth, but not companionship, that had been lacking all his life.

'I tell you what,' said Montagu. 'Instead of hanging around here waiting for Philip to get back from the hunt, why don't we show His Highness some of the art treasures now?'

'I would love that,' Charles said.

He sounded so boyish the others laughed. He was used to people laughing when he spoke and good-naturedly joined in. The mood of the party had been transformed, made buoyant, since Wat Montagu bounded in.

Montagu and Endymion led the way, though Buckingham too was familiar with the Escorial and its art treasures. The galleries were on the ground floor. They were larger, lighter and more extensive than at Whitehall. The heat beat in through the tiled walls, making the air dance with dust motes.

Endymion quietly assumed prominence as art guide, one of his many functions in Buckingham's household, and led Charles to what he knew the prince would like. There were paintings by Ribera, Zurbaran, Antonio Moro and Juan de las Ruelas. There was a magnificent portrait of the Duke de Lerma, minister to the Escorial's creator, Philip II, by Sánchez Coello.

'Do you know how many paintings they have here?' Charles asked Endymion.

'Over a thousand, your Highness. There are more in the other palaces, of course.'

'We have a lot of ca… ca… ca… catching up to do.'

'And we can do it,' Buckingham said.

Charles stopped in front of Titian's *Women With a Fur Coat*, stunned not only by the exposed single breast, the first he had ever seen, but by the transformative power of having a new and strange human being enter his soul and enrich it.

Then another Titian left him thunderstruck. This was the double portrait of Charles V and Isabella. Charles could hardly breathe. His stutter disappeared.

'Do you know the date of this?' For some reason he asked Wat Montagu, not Endymion.

Montagu supplied the date. '1548, Your Highness.'

'Call me Charles in private from now on.'

'Thank you, Charles. I would like that very much.'

'Yes. I do not need majesty in private. You see, Wat, that, there, is how you present majesty.' He nodded at the Titian, waving a hand at Charles V. 'Under Elizabeth majesty was presented as power, Protestant power. But that Titian presents majesty through love. Does it not? The king extends his majesty to all the subjects of the realm, embracing them in royal love.'

'Bravo! Well said, Charles!' Buckingham put an arm round his prince and kissed him.

'Thank you, George.'

Shortly afterwards a brightly liveried messenger found them and told them King Philip IV had returned from the hunt and awaited their pleasure. Endymion translated.

'Oh, so he's back then?' Buckingham stared haughtily at the messenger.

'Yes, Your Eminence.' The messenger bowed again, eyes to the floor.

'And he knew we were coming from Madrid today?'

'Yes, Your Eminence.'

'And he still went out bloody hunting?'

Endymion's translation made the message milder, but still the messenger made no reply.

'Well, did he or didn't he?'

'Yes, Your Eminence.'

Buckingham quoted Calmeta from Castiglione's *Book of the Courtier*: '"Look at the Spaniards, who appear to be the leaders in courtship, and consider how many are to be found who are extremely arrogant. They are worse than the French in so far as they first make a show of great modesty." That is what we are up against here, Charles.'

Endymion and Wat Montagu laughed. Charles looked horrified, gazing fearfully at the messenger, who still had his gaze fixed firmly on the ground. Fortunately, he had clearly not understood a word of what Buckingham had said.

The quartet of Englishmen, heady and happy in each other's company, were shown into the Royal Receiving Room to await the king. It was solid with richly inlaid tables with gold and silver ornaments on them. Nothing was functional; the only function was decoration. Rich tapestries completely covered every wall, no panelling was visible at all.

Some of these rich tapestries were surely the work of Raphael. Was that not a representation of Christ in a boat and the miraculous draught of fishes? Charles looked at the figures in the boat, bending, supplicating, stretching out their arms. It was a wonder.

Just before he left England, Charles had purchased a series of Raphael cartoons, *The Acts of the Apostles*, for the Mortlake tapestry factory. They were purchased as cartoons, rough drawings, to be worked into tapestries at Mortlake. Then they would hang in Inigo's new Banqueting House. These very Catholic works were to prepare London for the arrival of his Catholic bride, which he was now advancing.

Impatient as ever, Charles was already fretting at a possible delay to the work on the Raphael cartoons. Before he and Buckingham had left England, Francis Cleyn had been appointed to run the Mortlake Tapestry Works. Among the pile of letters waiting for Charles at the embassy was a notification that James had sent Cleyn, a German, back to the court of Christian IV, where he had come from, to obtain a letter clearing him to work at Mortlake. Charles was furious at James's typical pernickety, clerk-like, small-mindedness.

He turned back to beauty: On the wall facing him now, in the Royal Receiving Room, was a tapestry cycle of The *Conquest of Tunis*. They had been created for another Anglo-Spanish marriage, between Philip II and Mary Tudor. Their intention was to cow the Protestant English with a display of Habsburg military might.

His reverie at the *Conquest of Tunis* tapestries was interrupted by the Spanish king, who strode gracefully into his Receiving Room, trailing attendants, including Olivares and the seneschal, Don Fennyn.

Philip was seventeen years old. He had been king for only a year. Inigo had told Charles that he was well-read, as learned as James albeit so much younger. He had read Vetruvius, which counted heavily with Inigo. The extensive library, of which he was inordinately proud, housed works by Ovid, Euclid, Seneca and Aesop.

He was a tall, languorous-looking youth, blue eyed, with a pencil moustache and heavy jowls, strange on one so young. He was dressed from head to foot in black silk. He bore little resemblance to the portrait of his sister, the Infanta, which Charles had fallen in love with before he left England.

Charles thought Philip had a natural dignity which he, Charles, could aspire to but would sadly never reach. There was no apology for his absence when they arrived.

'Welcome, welcome.' Philip managed to smile and lisp at the same time. 'Such a pleasant surprise. We heard only recently that you were on the way.'

Endymion was translating. The group of Englishmen stood when Philip entered then resumed sitting. Buckingham, however, had managed to sprawl in an armchair with his feet up on a tabouret, an intricately upholstered small stool. He also kept his hat on. The magnificence of his attire – orange silk doublet and hose, white Spanish leather boots – did not mitigate the deliberate discourtesy which he managed to aim at Olivares.

Philip affected not to notice. He clicked his fingers. The seneschal, Don Fennyn, called for a host of footmen who entered with the welcome presents. Charles was presented with a great golden ewer set with precious stones and an entire cabinet of jewels. The Spanish queen had sent him a rich nightgown, gloves and sweet perfumes.

Olivares announced – in Spanish – there were to be acts of royal clemency in Charles's honour: the prisons were to be thrown open, the fines of miscreants paid and some death sentences commuted to life in prison.

Philip languidly waved away Charles's thanks for the effusive, if belated, welcome. 'There is an Indian legend,' he mused, smilingly, 'that there shall come visitors with flaxen hair, grey eyes and white complexions who shall govern us. They will be the heirs of Don Francisco Draco.' Philip laughed.

Charles, wide-eyed, understood for the first time the terror struck in the Spanish by the English privateers, Drake in the past and Raleigh to the present day.

'But today we know you, Prince Charles and milord Buckingham as great collectors of art. I hear you were looking at the paintings by Titian. I hope you will accept one as a welcome gift, my future brother-in-law. I thought perhaps the *Pardo Venus.*'

'Thank you. Thank you very much.' Charles resolved then and there to add as many Titians to his collection as he could.

'Not at all. The Titian is a noble painting. It shows the world of courtly love where carnal temptation in the form of the satyr is slain and Venus and true love reigns as Cupid flies above her, bow in hand.'

Buckingham snorted, perhaps thinking how far the English kingdom was from this ideal state. If Philip noticed he affected to ignore it.

'And tonight we have a feast for you and a play in your honour by our playwright of renown, Lope de Vega.'

'Thank you.' Charles wanted to ask if the Infanta would be at the feast and play but thought that sounded gauche. There was no sign of her now. In fact there were no women in the room at all.

'And I have one more gift of welcome for you Carlos Eduardo if it will please you.'

'Oh. Er. What?'

'I have arranged for our court painter to paint your portrait while you are with us. He has only just started here at court with us, still a young man, but we think rather highly of him. His name is Diego Velasquez.'

'Philip, you could not have thought of a better gift.' Charles was ecstatic. 'Thank you!'

Buckingham scowled. 'A portrait?' He glared at Philip. 'Your Majesty, how long do you think we are going to be here?'

That evening there was a banquet to welcome Charles. It was hosted by Philip with his lovely young queen, Elizabeth of France, who was Henri IV of France's daughter. Philip had changed for dinner and was resplendent in carnation satin embroidered with black and gold silk. At Charles's request, Endymion explained the orders he wore round his neck, the Toison d'Or and the cross of Santiago.

Charles was wearing his 'George', the Order of the Garter. He had donned a short cloak trimmed with fur and pearls, flung over his shoulder, a pair of baggy breeches of soft leather designed to hide the bowed curve of his legs, running down to white silk stockings over his calves, which made them look fuller. By his side hung a cup-hilted rapier in a jewelled scabbard.

Only Endymion had previously experienced the formality with which the meal was served. The tables were covered with cloths as rich as tapestries. Beating drums announced the arrival of phalanxes of servants in various liveries, who knelt down in waiting supplication with their eyes down before the call to serve the food. Only a call of 'mozo' brought them to their feet to await instruction.

Endymion and Wat Montagu explained each course of food to Charles. There was olla podrida, the national dish of chicken in a pot; garbanzos – peas and beans with bacon; an estofado of veal; fried river trout; poached eggs; a quisado of rabbit; fried sausages; chicken and rice; and a Montaches ham. There were flagons of delicious val-de-peñas wine, which Philip, an attentive, smiling host, assured them could be drunk in limitless quantities without getting drunk.

Charles gobbled away, eating far more than he did at home and getting mildly drunk, despite Philip's assurances about the wine. Buckingham's mood did not improve. To Olivares's open amusement he had developed toothache.

After the meal, a play was performed in the King's Receiving Room for the Prince's amusement. Only the royal party were seated on chairs, the ladies sat on Turkey carpets and the few courtiers admitted stood modestly in the background. One of the ladies was openly eying Buckingham, first his famous calves then his handsome face. When Endymion whispered to Buckingham that this was Olivares's wife, Buckingham turned in his seat and gave her a beautiful smile. For a moment, his toothache left him.

The Lope de Vega play, as Philip explained, was especially written for the occasion. It celebrated the coming of 'Carlos Eduardo' and his forthcoming nuptials. More of a scene than a play, the brief drama centred on a brave knight who travels far to woo his true love.

Then, just as Charles was dozing off from the unaccustomed quantity of wine, the aim of his travels and the object of his desire entered the room. The Infanta Anna was accompanied by a redoubtable duenna of permanent-looking middle-age, armoured in black bombazine. Endymion whisperingly identified her as Doña Elvira de Mandanilla. The duenna carried a mandolin, holding it stiffly in front of her, staring round with a sharp gaze as if wary that the unaccustomed foreign guests might purloin or break the instrument.

Charles remembered he had been in love with the Infanta for some time and made an effort to feel stirred, moved. To feel *something*.

The Infanta Anna was sixteen but looked much younger. As a first impression, she looked more Flemish than Spanish. She certainly bore little resemblance to the portrait he had been sent. There was no resemblance, either, to the beauteous Anne of Austria, her sister.

Charles glanced anxiously at Buckingham. At the sight of the girl, his face had dropped into that stiff mask he wore to conceal emotion. He was suffering. Charles wanted to help him but did not know how to. He resumed a determined effort to be the romantic courtly lover of this ordinary looking girl.

She wore a simply embroidered jacket and a long full skirt. Her only ornament was a single oleander in her hair. She was certainly comely; it would perhaps be unkind to say plump. Charles fought his impression of too much flesh. She was fair-haired, with beautifully pencilled eyebrows and a pink and white complexion which reddened when she noticed Charles looking at her. Even to Charles's inexperienced eye, her emotion was nearer embarrassment or even distress than interest, let alone love or affection.

Doña Elvira de Mandanilla passed the mandolin to her charge, seconds before she was to play it. The Infanta

Anna played and passably sang a Spanish air unfamiliar even to Endymion.

Wat Montagu whispered a rough translation of the song into Charles's ear. It was about a Spanish maiden who was carried off by a moor, but after long captivity was rescued by her knightly lover. The theme of the evening was becoming clear.

Her duty done, the Infanta Anna fled, trailing her middle-aged duenna, who struggled to keep up.

'Bravo!' said Buckingham. He applauded, ironically. Nobody else followed him.

CHAPTER 10
*CARLOS EDUARDO SOY!*

Even to himself, Charles's attempts to approach the Infanta came to resemble a Comedia del Arte farce more than the picaresque Quixotic adventure he had seen himself playing in when he started his journey.

Soon after that first night, he had been told the Infanta would be taking a carriage ride round the Prado. Charles took Wat Montagu with him in a royal caroche, but the Infanta drove off as soon as she saw him. Wat Montague counselled against pursuit.

At least the crowds were friendly. Charles was recognised and they burst into a snatch of the play Lope de Vega had written, performed on his first night.

> *Carlos Eduardo soy*
> *Que, scindo Amor mi quia*
> *El cielo d'España voy*
> *Per ver mi estrella Maria*

Wat translated it for him: "'Charles Stuart I am. Love has guided me far. To the heaven of Spain. To Maria my star." Isn't Spanish beautiful? I prefer it even to French.'

Charles pouted at Wat Montagu. He wanted the day with him to last forever, so he could stay happy. He was secretly relieved the Infanta had bolted at the sight of him.

His next attempt at approaching the Infanta came some two weeks later. By then, Olivares had told him he may not have a private interview with her, even if accompanied by the redoubtable duenna, until negotiations were much more advanced and the wedding was about to be announced.

Charles consulted Endymion about a clandestine meeting, like Romeo and Juliet. Endymion smiled, not unkindly. He told Charles the Infanta visited her confessor, Padre Ambrosio, every week before celebrating vespers at the Monastery of Recoletos Agustinos, at the western end of the Prado Palace. Before her confession, she took a walk in the gardens of the monastery, sometimes even eluding the duenna. Charles resolved to come upon her as if by accident in the garden, there to woo her and fall in love.

'Are you familiar with a story by the name of *La Celestina*?' Charles asked Wat Montagu, 'Endymion loaned me his translation of it.'

The usual grin broke out. 'I know it's a Spanish classic by Fernando de Rojas but I'm afraid I haven't read it.'

'Ah! Well. The hero, Calisto, approaches his beloved, Malibea, in a garden and professes his love.'

'How does it turn out?'

'Celisto is killed when he falls from a ladder leading to Melibea's window.'

Wat Montagu laughed. 'That doesn't sound very promising, does it?'

'N... n... no, not really. Calisto and Melibea are brought together by a bawd by the name of La Celestina. Hence the title.'

'That is my role, is it? The bawd?' The grin broke out again.'

'Mmm. She was quite a n... n... nice bawd.'

By now, Charles felt more comfortable in Wat Montagu's company than he did alone. He had always fretted when alone; without Elizabeth, in the early days, then without Henry, finally without Buckingham. But he had never felt as close to anyone as he was with Wat Montagu.

He was excited by their coming adventure together, dressing with some care for the occasion in the court suit he had worn in Paris – white velvet doublet and hose flashed with azure silk. He topped that with a broad-brimmed

Spanish hat adorned with a diamond brooch and a white dropping plume.

But a problem arose. Charles and a broadly grinning Wat Montagu could find no way into the garden. The doors were locked. When they heard the Infanta on the other side of the wall, apparently talking to herself or perhaps praying, Charles decided to climb the wall that separated them – a romantic gesture.

By now, the escapade was more Pyramus and Thisbe than Romeo and Juliet, but Charles was determined so a grinning Wat Montagu hoisted the small and surprisingly light figure of his prince to the top of the wall. Charles scrambled up and dropped over, falling on the other side almost on top of the Infanta, who screamed 'Madre santissima' then fled, still screaming.

Charles had hurt his fragile ankle, had lost his plumed hat and muddied and torn his white suit. He sat on the grass, winded, while Wat Montagu called anxiously from the other side of the wall.

Eventually, a gardener appeared, accompanied by the redoubtable duenna, who was evidently never far away. They unlocked one of the doors to the garden ushering Charles wordlessly through, then hastily locking it again. Wat Montagu half carried, half led him back to their caroche.

Charles's next glimpses of the elusive Infanta were on more formal occasions. The Spanish had offered extravagant hospitality. This had included evenings of fireworks, torch-lit processions and chivalric games which reminded Charles of poor dead Henry's valour. There were also ballets and plays at the Puerta del Sol. Here, the scene-changes, to Charles's great interest, were better than they had been in France, though to his mind still not quite as ingenious as those of Inigo.

There were also bullfights at the Plaza Mayor, hunting trips for wild boar, wolf and fox in the El Pardo royal domain, celebratory processions from San Geronimo past splendid buildings – even the Common Prison looked like a palace – and feasts of unbridled plenty.

At all of these the Infanta – as stiffly rigid as an Elizabethan portrait – was glimpsed at various distances. But requests to meet her, even heavily chaperoned, were blocked behind a wall of Spanish obstructive courtesy, usually led by Olivares.

Endymion was working all the daylight hours and into the night, needing all the reserves of his fabled sweet temper to see him through the strain. He was the sole translator for the negotiations, sometimes going back to the embassy in Madrid to collect any letters and parcels from England.

Somehow, in these short breaks back in Madrid, he also found time to look after the Ambassador, John Digby's ten-year-old son, George, an inquisitive boy with fair hair and large blue eyes. Endymion took the much-ignored boy on trips round the markets, to bullfights and even to taverns for watered red wine.

They were sometimes accompanied by Henry Jermyn. Jermyn was officially another translator, but at seventeen John Digby pronounced him too young for access to delicate negotiations. He was therefore left kicking his heels at the embassy with nothing to do.

One broiling day in high summer, Endymion was ordered away from the deadlocked negotiations to guide Charles and Buckingham round the Madrid *pinturas* – picture dealers. Endymion suggested that they also visit some *almonedas* – estate sales – where one could pick up art at bargain prices. At Charles's fervent insistence Wat Montagu accompanied them.

They visited a court official, Don Jerónimo Funes y Muñoz. He lived on a large estate just outside Madrid. At his *almonedas*, Charles chose five paintings and Buckingham three. Charles's selection included a painting by Carracci, the tiny but exquisite *Agony in the Garden*, and by Adam Elsheimer, *Witch Riding Backwards on a Goat*, which was an oil on copper, something Charles had not seen before.

Buckingham, in rare good humour at being away from Olivares and near art, traced the influence of Dürer, who Charles had only the vaguest idea of, on Adam Elsheimer. He clapped Charles on the shoulder, sending the prince spinning. 'You know something Baby Charles, even my bloody toothache has cleared. We should do this more often.'

Their host, Don Jerónimo Funes y Muñoz, was keen to show them the contents of his Wunderkammer, something that always reminded Charles of Henry, whose collection of coins and artefacts he admired but did not intend to emulate. Don Jerónimo too had a coin collection, which did not interest the visiting Englishmen greatly, along with a collection of silverware and weapons, which included swords, crossbows and arquebuses. Everything here, indeed everything on the entire estate, appeared to be for sale.

Charles bought eight silver candlesticks, more handsomely worked than anything he had seen in England. Endymion was looking at everything keenly.

'Do you want to buy something for little Charles?' Buckingham said softly to him.

Endymion hesitated. He thought back to Charles Porter's birth. Buckingham had refused him permission to return to his estate at Woodhall to be with Olive at the birth. He needed Endymion, so he said, for a diplomatic mission to Rubens in Antwerp. Olive had nearly lost the baby, though both she and Charles were well now.

'Do you think he would like this dagger?' Buckingham said sotto voce to Endymion. The dagger had a jewelled handle and would cost a fortune.

'My Lord...'

'Allow me to advance the sum,' Buckingham said. He put an arm round Endymion's shoulders. 'I behaved badly three years ago but let me make amends now. You know my choler, my friend. My choler is my curse. But if ever you wanted revenge for my behaviour, Endymion, you have it now. I am suffering the torments of the damned in this benighted country.'

Endymion was emboldened by the confession. 'You mean...?'

'Yes, Endymion, I mean the woman who tortures my nights even though I have the fairest and most loving wife on God's sweet earth. Who could compose such exquisite torture? So let me be of use, Endymion. Young Charles Porter is to have his dagger.'

There were tears in Endymion's eyes. 'Thank you, my Lord. And I shall tell my Charles when he is old enough how good a man his patron is.'

They fell into each other's arms. Both of them weeping.

After this first success, they visited several estate sales in the Manzanares valley in and around Madrid. Endymion knew Madrid as well as London; he knew where to go and what to buy. At one estate sale he bought a work by a little-known Spanish painter, Caxes, a copy of *The Chastity of Joseph*, and a Dürer drawing.

He spent nearly £200 on paintings for his London home and his country place, Woodhall in the Cotswolds, despite having no income other than his salary from Buckingham. He spent an even greater percentage of his money on art than even Buckingham and Charles did. But his beloved Olive had a new petticoat and waistcoat every month. There was always enough money for that, Endymion made sure of it.

Charles bought avidly, leaving payment to Buckingham and arrangements to Endymion. His haul included another

Titian, by now his most beloved painter. This was the *Allegory of the Marquis of Vasto*. Like Titian's *Woman in a Fur Coat* it added to Charles's limited knowledge of the female breast, but the mystery element in this allegory also intrigued him. He resolved to have it copied, so he could study it during this lengthy stay in Spain, while the original was protected at home.

He also bought Andrea del Sarto's *Madonna and Child* and Tintoretto's *Christ Washing the Feet of the Apostles*. He was just earnestly discussing the Tintoretto with Wat Montagu, when he noticed Endymion warmly greeting one of the Spaniards at the estate sale. Charles abruptly broke off his conversation with Wat and stood uneasily in front of Endymion until he was introduced.

'Your Highness, this is señor Juan Gómez de Mora.'

The Spaniard gave a suitably courtly stiff bow, muttering, 'Your Highness, it is my honour.'

But Charles was hopping from foot to foot with excitement. Before setting off to Spain Charles had read widely, as well as attempting to learn Spanish.

One of the books he read was Cabrera's history of Philip II's life. Along with Charles V, Philip II was the creative spirit of the Habsburg dynasty, into which Charles would be marrying, when these negotiations finally finished. Charles found both Charles V and Philip II attractive figures to emulate, despite their Catholicism. Indeed, some aspects of what he admired in them were inseparable from Catholicism.

Philip II was also a great builder, as Charles hoped to be with Inigo's invaluable help. Philip II had moved the capital of Spain from the narrow winding alleys of Toledo to the open boulevards and squares of Madrid. The Madrid Charles was enjoying at the moment was a recent creation. The Escorial, the hunting lodge, El Pardo, the palace at Aranjuez were all relatively new.

But above all, the magnificent square of the Plaza Mayor, although designed by Philip II's architect, Juan de Herrera, had been started some seven years ago and finished only five years ago by the very señor Juan Gómez de Mora who now stood in front of him. His father had been court painter to Philip II.

The bull-fight Charles had been taken to as part of the celebrations at his arrival had been at the amphitheatre especially built at the Plaza Mayor. Indeed, Charles now remembered seeing de Mora there on that occasion, though he had not been introduced and Charles did not know who he was.

Charles had often been back to the square since then, in the weeks, now becoming months, he had been in Madrid. He had attended masques, fetes and on one occasion a public execution. The terrible auto-de-fés, the public burnings, had also taken place in the square, as Buckingham reminded him from time to time, when he thought Charles was softening on Catholicism.

Charles was babbling in his excitement. 'My dear... señor de Mora. I must congratulate you on that magnificent... Surely the most superb square in Europe?'

After Endymion had translated de Mora smilingly replied, 'I hope so, Your Highness. I believe it is certainly the largest square in Europe.'

'I... I have so many questions. In England, I have a superb architect of my own, Inigo Jones. We hope one day to... to... create something of the same order of magnificence in London. Tell me, what of habitations? Did you have to clear surrounding habitations?'

De Mora, who looked around forty and was dressed in court black, gave a slight smile. 'Oh yes, Your Highness. All the habitations had to be cleared from the whole area.'

'And it is unpaved. Interesting um um...'

Charles did not notice but Endymion was looking serious. Buckingham was frowning. So bound up was

Charles with his new friend he even failed to notice that Wat Montagu had taken over the translation.

'Yes, Your Highness. It is unpaved. We sand it sometimes.'

'Do you still have the plans? I must study the plans. I... I... shall write to Inigo about them. I shall visit you, if I may. I shall come to your studio.'

Endymion touched the architect lightly on the arm in warning. De Mora nodded in acknowledgement. 'I can bring the plans to you at the Escorial, Your Highness. It will be my honour to discuss them with you if Your Highness so wishes.'

The meeting was arranged for the next day. Buckingham was involved in negotiations with Olivares and Endymion was translating, so only Wat Montagu was present in Charles's suite at the Escorial when de Mora arrived. Over wine and cakes, the architect explained the construction of the four facades of the plaza, each of them surrounded by porticos, quite unheard of in England. There were stately archways open onto the streets by which the plaza is approached.

Charles asked if he could have a copy of the plans. He then dictated a letter to Wat Montagu who wrote it in fair script in Spanish. The letter invited de Mora to London, to work on the new Whitehall Palace with Inigo Jones and to construct a plaza like the Plaza Mayor in London.

When the invitation became known, the Spanish courtly manner vanished instantly. They erupted with rage. Olivares, the past-master of delaying, used the incident to break off negotiations over the marriage completely.

Buckingham threatened to take Charles home. By now, Buckingham and Olivares hardly entered the same room at the same time. They were at opposite ends of the Escorial and sent messengers. Endymion was shuttling from one to the other, smoothing ruffled feathers. Olivares involved Philip. The letter of invitation to de Mora had to be formally withdrawn, in writing, though Buckingham bluntly refused to have Charles apologise.

Charles and Wat Montagu had taken to visiting the monastery at San Geronimo, from where the Spanish kings used to make their way into the capital for their coronation. It was in an anonymous area just outside central Madrid where they attracted no attention. Without telling Buckingham or even Endymion they sometimes quietly took part in Catholic services and ceremonials there.

They were at Vespers, sitting quietly and unnoticed at the back of the chapel. Something about the atmosphere, the beauty of it all, the peace and calm caused Wat Montagu to open his heart to his new friend Charles.

Speaking in a monotone, not looking Charles in the eye, Wat spoke of the severe beatings he received at the hands of his father, a fervent puritan. The beatings had become even worse since Sir Henry had been demoted to President of the Council, losing favour with James. He had taken up self-flagellation, as well as beating Edward, Wat's older brother, but mainly the younger, smaller Wat.

As Vespers opened, with the priest before the altar draped with a beautiful green cloth saying 'Deus, in adiutorium meum intende' the congregation took up the words chanting with him. 'Domine, ad adiuvandum me festina.'

And then the Antiphon, Salve Regina Caelorum. As Charles knew, it was sung at the end of Compline and Vespers. There came the image of the Virgin as the mother of light: Salve Radix, salve porta/ Ex qua mundo lux est orta. (Hail the root, hail the gateway/ Through which the light of the world was born.)

As Charles and Wat Montagu were subsumed in the beauty of holiness, a shaft of evening sunlight broke through the stained glass window, alighting on the symbol of the Holy Spirit, behind the altar. The symbol was a dove, the Paraclete, the intercessor. It was raised above seven ranges of clouds. In the clouds were welcoming archangels, cherubim, seraphim.

To Wat Montagu, God's sign to him could not have been clearer. As the Paraclete became golden in its sunbeam rays he whispered to Charles. 'I shall become a Catholic. In my heart I feel I have become one already.'

Charles puffed out his cheeks. 'Have you told this to… to…'

Wat smiled his handsome smile. His compact frame looked at ease. 'Only you.'

'Best keep it under your hat. Olivares would make great play…'

'I know.'

Then Wat and Charles lost themselves in the singing of the Magnificat.

# CHAPTER 11
## *DIEGO VELAZQUEZ*

Charles's portrait sessions with Diego Velazquez started, as Philip had promised, soon after his and Buckingham's arrival at the Escorial. The newly-minted Court Painter, appointed by Olivares with Philip's blessing, had been given a studio in one of the galleries, the Gallery of the North Wind.

It was long and narrow, windowed along its length, facing north to catch the dry, blue Madrid light. In the distance the painter could see the snow-capped peak of La Meliciosa. There was a pungent smell of linseed oil. Velazquez was so new he had not yet managed to establish his own smell in his own studio.

Some of the painter's early works from his days in Seville were stacked along the walls. They were mainly *bodegónes* – ordinary people eating and drinking, a genre the Dutch did so well. The change to elevated court paintings would be a challenge.

Endymion had warned Charles that the temperamental artist was not happy. Only just off the coach from Seville, he felt like a clodhopping provincial in the glorious capital. He had also been promised the commission of painting His Majesty. This had been postponed. He had been told to paint the English Prince Charles instead.

As soon as he had been told to paint Prince Charles it started to rain. It rained for days, as apparently it often did, here in the capital. Who was this Prince Charles? Velazquez had no idea. Some sort of foreign heretic, apparently.

When he first set eyes on Charles, the painter was near apoplectic, waving his arms and gibbering to himself. How was he to make a regal portrait from such unpromising stuff? Nobody could mould a pot if the clay was defective.

And if he failed? Almost as soon as he arrived, Velazquez had discovered a cellar deep in the bowels of the Escorial where they jettisoned unwanted paintings. It was a graveyard of art, canvases waiting to be re-used or even destroyed; failed princes, kings insufficiently flattered, disproportionate queens, shaky drapery. This was his first commission. Mother of God, what if it ended up in the cellar, the purgatory of art hell?

Velazquez's depths of rage were obvious enough from his manner, but his depths of misery were even greater. Just before leaving Seville, Velazquez had married the daughter of his master, Francisco Pacheco, with an ample dowry. Pacheco, who Velazquez adored, was to come to him when he was settled in the capital. This, too, was now in limbo until a portrait of this misshapen foreign heretic could be completed.

Could the fate of Diego Velazquez become any worse after looking so promising on his appointment to the Spanish court? The answer was yes it could. The sitter, this Prince Charles, was constantly called away, not to the negotiations in which he played no part, but to carouse, take part in processions, attend the plays at Corral de la Cruz or visit bullfights at Plaza Mayor and – God preserve us – buy paintings from artists other than Diego Velazquez.

Diego Velazquez has sinned against God. That is the only explanation. For not only is he condemned to paint a frequently-absent heretic midget, said midget will not shut up. He burbles and stammers away in French, requiring the artist, he, Diego Velazquez, to explain every step of his procedure as he is proceeding with it.

It is a wonder the artist can still hold a brush, having to paint under these conditions. It would take the playwright Don Pedro to render his sufferings and then the audience at the Plaza Mayor would weep for him.

But he has a plan. Diego Velazquez has a plan. He intends to murder the Protestant dwarf, then tell His

Majesty it would be a heresy to paint a corpse, so can he please now proceed with the original plan and paint His Majesty? Thank you.

Charles thought the portrait sessions with Velazquez were going rather well. He knew from Endymion that the painter was exactly the same age as himself. He had remarked on that fact at their first session but Velazquez had not replied. He was a haughty yet nervy fellow, enigmatic and self-contradictory. In appearance, he was broad-shouldered, with extravagantly upturned waxed moustaches and fleshy lips.

At first, he had affected not to speak French but eventually a reply was pulled from the painter in that language, rather in the manner of hauling the gizzards from a dead chicken before cooking it, a procedure Charles and Elizabeth had witnessed more than once during their upbringing in Scotland.

After a while, Velazquez did not seem to mind explaining what he was doing as he was doing it. Charles tried to put him at ease, realising he was overawed by a Prince from mighty England. And his procedures really were quite interesting, very different from Daniel Mytens, for example, James's court painter, who was the last artist to paint Charles.

Velazquez did many nervous chalk sketches as preparation. Then he took a regular weave canvas, pre-stretched by boys employed for the purpose. He lathered the canvas with dark brown ground, using sweeping strokes from a palette knife. Charles asked him why he did not use a lighter ground but there was no reply.

Then he blocked in the main composition with a large bristle brush. There were no lines, as Charles would have expected, just blocks of light and shade. Then the blocks of colour were worked using softer brushes, then a blending brush, then for the finest details a really fine pointed brush apparently of ermine or stoat. As he painted, he frequently wiped his brush clean on the canvas. Charles had never seen anything like that before. He asked the painter about this curious habit but there was no reply.

Velazquez decided to paint Charles in armour. This would help make him look bigger and disguise his various physical problems, especially his legs. A warrior, then, not a lover. As a wedding portrait for the Infanta Anna a warrior was just as good as a lover.

Charles was depicted with his right arm resting on a globe – conqueror of worlds, ha-ha-ha – and in that hand he holds a baton, as fingers are the very devil to paint even in gloves. The left arm is leaning upon the hip, being partly supported by the hilt of the sword. Charles had appeared wearing an order which obviously meant a great deal to him. This, Velazquez learned from his voluble subject, was the Order of St George. So that was included.

If the subject was wearing armour and an order of chivalry there had to be a battle in the background. Velazquez had no idea what battles, if any, the heretic had been involved in. He hoped none of them were against Catholics. But he painted something safe, a generic siege with numerous figures engaged in storming a town which he based on Seville because that was easiest.

There was drapery because there had to be drapery, and anyway it was quick. The drapery was done using a yellow ground, crossed by stripes of red. It was behind the figure, with the curtain covering one half of the globe on which the right arm rested.

When Charles first looked at the completed painting he was struck by how thin the colour was. Velazquez had put linseed oil into the pigment to thin it. It was also not glazed as highly as Charles was used to. It looked as if the paint had been floated on. There were signs of haste, a disregard for detail. The drapery was too simple, not the swirls and whorls he would have expected. And then he looked again and it was not too simple at all. With few folds, it gave a sense of largeness with telling broad shadows.

There was an aerial perspective on the battle, giving the impression of Charles rising above the fighting. That was emphasised by his gleaming, almost ethereal black armour. There was no obvious artifice, it simply was so. The viewer does not perceive the obstacles the artist has surmounted. Charles nodded his head at the rectitude of this.

And then he took a first look at the representation of his body. The hand position was like Paul van Somer's portrait of Henry, displayed at Hampton Court. This echo of Henry was pure chance – it was a not uncommon pose – but it pleased Charles.

Charles's eye roamed over the portrait, then he understood why the eye was being given this freedom. There was no white in the portrait at all. White lead would draw the eye to a certain place, without it the viewer was everywhere.

It had been painted de *primero mano* – dashed off – the tones blended while they were still wet. But somehow everything led to the face.

Charles looked at his face, as rendered by Diego Velazquez. At first glance, the expression is tranquil; the easy conqueror. The Spanish artist showed him with a full beard, covering his cheeks, not with whiskers shaved showing only a pointed beard as was the fashion at the Spanish court. But that full beard illuminated something of Charles. It showed his need to hide, to retreat into himself or to hide behind someone stronger.

Truth not art gave that face its harmony. The painter instinctively read the soul of the stranger thrust upon him. The unhappy prince was shown with full, liquid eyes calmly resting beneath the high, expansive, intelligent forehead. Bushy brows veil occasional temper born of fear for the self. There is some pride and much obstinacy. More, there is a fatal inactivity and incapacity for action.

This is a man whose mind can conceive and suggest, not receive or judge well. This is a mind never without a plan, usually several plans. This is a soul that was never without hope.

At that moment, in the studio with the unhappy painter forgotten, Charles disappeared into Velazquez's view of himself, never to return. He came to realise something he never forgot. Velazquez had painted not an idealized view of himself, not an enhanced view of himself but he had created the emergent Charles that Charles could one day be.

Those stages in the creation of the portrait that Charles had watched – the chalk sketches, the blocks of colour – were like the emergence from chrysalis as he tried to be Charles. But the finished work was not Charles. It was more than Charles.

Velazquez's genius, almost despite the painter's own self, had not merely represented Charles, he had created him. No mimesis in paint here, but the artist as God moulding a breathing man where before there was only clay.

Baby Charles died in that studio and Charles Stuart the man was born. He may not yet know who he was, but at least he knew what he looked like. In gratitude, Charles left a munificent hundred ducats with the seneschal for Velazquez. Velazquez took it with relief rather than gratitude. He was delighted to see the back of Charles.

# CHAPTER 12
## *A GAME AT CHESS*

Negotiations started slowly then slowed down. The Spanish naturally operated at a stately pace, which, as they knew very well, infuriated Buckingham. They forever sought delay. Charles and Buckingham were prisoners in a gilded cage, a situation of their own making. The Spanish needed only to wait to wear them down.

As Sir John Digby had forecast when Charles and Buckingham first arrived, the Spanish had involved the Pope, first Gregory XV then his successor, Urban XIII. They had also appointed a junta of theologians which delayed negotiations even more, as it was meant to.

The junta finally pronounced that Charles must remain in Spain for a year after the wedding ceremony. Also, complete freedom of worship for Catholics in England must be not only enshrined in law but actively enforced. Buckingham let loose a volley of curses at that which Endymion struggled to render more mildly in translation.

None of this especially perturbed Charles, as he was happy in Spain. His rejections by the Infanta mattered so little he was surprised himself at his indifference. It was very different for Buckingham.

Still plagued by toothache, loathing the heat, Buckingham feared for his life if he was away from England too long. His enemies, mainly the Somerset faction, had been plotting against him before he left. James could find a new handsome bed-fellow at any time. Probably only his rapidly deteriorating health had stopped him doing so already.

Buckingham's only joy lay in baiting Olivares. Negotiations had stopped altogether at one point when Olivares accused Buckingham of being in alliance with the French and not wanting the marriage at all. Almost as an afterthought, he accused him of having designs on his wife.

'Did you seduce his wife, my Lord?' an amused Wat Montagu asked his employer.

Buckingham gave a rare smile. 'No, I did something far worse than that, Wat. I brought her to the point when she was pleading for it then didn't seduce her.'

Even the straight-laced Charles laughed at that.

There was a real fear among the English, including the staff at the embassy, that the Spanish would, in the politest possible way, not let them go at all. In August, some five months after they arrived, an English fleet was sent to collect Charles at Santander.

Charles, Buckingham, Endymion and Wat Montagu bade a hasty goodbye to Philip and set off before anybody could stop them. Nevertheless, Philip gave Charles farewell presents including a sword and dagger set with diamonds and a set of rapiers of Toledo steel.

They left by night, muffled in their cloaks, hats pulled down to disguise their features, each carrying a dark lantern beneath his mantle. Their carriage drove to the Prado and then along the footpath leading to the Puerta de Recoletos. There, there was a monument the Spanish had erected in celebration of the marriage. The marriage was never called off, it was merely permanently in abeyance.

The four Englishmen reached Santander without let or hindrance. But a tempest blew up; the English ships swayed at anchor. As they boarded the *Defiance*, Charles fell off the gangplank into the sea. He could not swim and had to be rescued from drowning by the captain himself, Sir Sackville Trevor, diving into the turbid waters after him.

James was too ill to meet them at Dover. They set off for his palace at Royston, where they found him taken to his bed, racked with rheumatism, too ill even to go hunting. There was open speculation about how long he would last.

Back in London, Endymion and Wat Montagu were both made Groom of the Bedchamber to Charles, transferring from Buckingham's staff to Charles's with Buckingham's blessing. Buckingham also took charge of Velazquez's painting of Charles, hanging it in his London home, York House. The portrait reminded Charles of the Infanta, now an embarrassing memory.

The memory did not last long. All London, indeed all England, was in uproar. Charles and Buckingham had become Protestant heroes for failing to arrange a marriage with the Catholic Infanta. In celebration, the privateers were joyfully let loose to attack and plunder Spanish shipping.

Thomas Middleton wrote a most ingenious play about the Stuart dynasty's popular diplomatic failure. It ran for over a week; a great theatrical success. Accounts of it were dispatched to Madrid, as well as to Florence, Rome and Venice. Its fame was spread throughout England by prints of the script carried by riders from William Peake's print shop in the Strand.

Middleton's *A Game at Chess* was performed by The King's Men at the Globe. When Charles and Buckingham went to see the play they were swept up by the sabre-rattling euphoria the play was both creating and fanning. Both were in farouche mood, sporting the ridiculous false beards they had worn when they set out to Spain. They could hardly stop laughing and did not wish to.

At a packed-to-heaving Globe, they did not take a box, according to their rank and station, but stood among the groundlings, where they were quickly recognised and cheered to the rafters. They acknowledged the applause with solemn bows and a low sweep of their hats.

*A Game at Chess* dramatized a conflict between Spain and England as a game of chess. The players were all chess pieces and the drama involved some real chess moves. On the white side there was England: Charles was the White Knight, Buckingham was the White Duke, who moved like a knight. Charles's sister, Elizabeth of Bohemia, as she was becoming known, was the White Queen and James was the White King. On the black side, Philip of Spain was the Black King, the Infanta Maria was the Black Queen and Olivares was the Black Duke.

The white side were portrayed as pure and heroic, except for James as the White King. The author, Thomas Middleton, was a close friend of Sir Thomas Overbury. Overbury was a lover of Robert Carr, James's great favourite before Buckingham. He was also a lover of James's, who, James felt, had slighted him in some way.

To be rid of Overbury James ordered him to Moscow as ambassador to the court of Michael of Russia. Overbury refused to go. In a fit of rage, James had him sent to the Tower, where he died. In revenge, Overbury's friend Middleton portrayed James in the play as a doddering old lecher. James's expected imminent death may have emboldened him.

But all was praise for Charles as the White Knight and Buckingham as the White Duke. They travelled to the Black House, meaning Spain, for complicated negotiations involving an accusation of rape of the White Queen, symbolising Elizabeth's loss of Bohemia and the Palatinate. The Back Court was decorated with statues, candles, crosses and other symbols of Popish idolatry.

In the end, the Black King and the Black Duke admitted their crimes. But by this time the theatre was in uproar with the audience more interested in the flesh and blood heroes among them than they were in seeing an account of them on stage. Charles and Buckingham were swept up shoulder high and carried to a place of honour on stage, their false beards long lost in the melee.

Next day, the Spanish Ambassador protested to James about the play, giving him a lurid account of it. James had the play shut after one more performance. A warrant went out for Middleton's arrest. He went into hiding. To force him to break cover, his son Edward was arrested. Middleton surrendered himself and was thrown into the Fleet. He was eventually released on a promise to James that he would no longer write plays.

A messenger came from James's palace at Royston the day after Charles and Buckingham saw Middleton's play. When the messenger was announced, Charles assumed he was bringing news of James's death, but he was not.

The letter was from James, still very much alive. It told him about a young girl who he vaguely remembered. She looked about thirteen years old, as he recalled. She had danced for him at the Louvre, paying more attention to him than to Buckingham.

Ah yes! He pictured it again. She had danced the role of one of Circe's attendant dryads. She was a tiny, skinny girl with a toothy grin wearing a diaphanous green-blue dress. She had kicked off her cork soled shoes, he pictured that.

According to James's message, this girl was the sister of the French king, Louis XIII. Her name was Henrietta-Maria. He was to marry her. She brought a dowry of 800,000 crowns. Apparently, that had done the trick.

# CHAPTER 13
## MURDER MOST FOUL

Finally, James Stuart was dying. This, Buckingham thought sardonically, had taken an unconscionably long time. He had hoped for news of James's death throughout the endless hot days in Spain, to rescue him from the company of the toad Olivares. But no.

Buckingham thought of the Daniel Mytens portrait of James. There he was in all his pomp, sitting enthroned in the red and silver garter robes of state with emblazoned motto – Beati Pacifici. It had been painted two years before the Spanish trip and he looked like an embalmed corpse even then. His face under his dyed-black hair was a taut death mask polished up with rouge. Mytens had defiantly showed his right foot twisted, indicating the rickets which had plagued him all his life and which he had passed on to Charles.

What kept James alive, in Buckingham's opinion, was the need, before he died, to wreak vengeance on anybody who had ever slighted him. James's driving humour was bile. His violations of Buckingham were acts of bitter rage.

In the same spirit, he wanted to vent his fury on Frances Howard and Robert Carr before he left this earth. The two of them wished to marry. His hatred of the Countess of Essex ran the deepest. Frances had thwarted him, fooled him and made a poltroon of him at the Tethys Festival masque.

She had been betrothed to her husband, the Earl of Essex, Robert Devereux, when she was fourteen and he was thirteen. She claimed the marriage had not been consummated and so was void. Frances now wished to marry Robert Carr, as she thought she could remould him and make something of him. The sometime favourite fell passionately in love with her, which he was unable to dissemble or hide from an enraged James.

Robert Carr and Frances sought permission to marry. James took his revenge by demanding that Frances take a near public virginity test first, to prove Devereux had not penetrated her.

The test was to be attended by no fewer than ten matrons and two midwives. It took all Buckingham's tact and charm to stop James putting in a leering appearance himself, the greater to humiliate her. The assembled ladies found Frances's hymen intact. She and Carr were permitted to marry. But the king had had his revenge. He could now embrace welcome death.

Enfeebled in mind and body, he lay in a huge bed at Theobalds, where Henry had died, while a March wind howled outside, rattling on the windows as if summoning James to his maker.

He was thought to be suffering from a tertian ague which gave him shaking fits, first hot then cold, with ravings and prickling sensations. He also had dysentery, which left the once white sheets soiled and stinking as fast as they could be changed. But the pain raging in his twisted joints, causing him to buck and howl, was gout. He had not been able to walk for weeks and had been carried to Theobalds in a litter.

Sir Theodore Mayerne had diplomatically absented himself from a scene where he could bring neither cure nor comfort. He had taken a trip back to his hometown of Geneva, making sure he was out of reach of messages.

James's personal physician, Sir William Paddy, now in his seventies, had put in an appearance but could only recommend praying for James's soul. A forlorn hope, Buckingham thought to himself as he composed his features into a mask of sadness.

James's treatments were seen as cooling and moist to counter the hot and dry humour of tertian ague. But he loathed taking any medicines, especially purgatives. So his clysters, juleps, cooling epithems, plasters, ointments, poultices and all the rest of it lay untouched on an oak table beside his bed.

Buckingham stared coolly at the failing nostrums as if in league with them. The doctors had abandoned the scene of their defeat. James had sent the footmen and servants away, as their fluttering ministrations irritated him. Only Buckingham remained of the courtiers and nobles.

He had taken over the role of Groom of the Stool from the Earl of Kellie, adding to his myriad other offices and titles, especially to preside over the stinking near-corpse in his death throes. He did not wish to be near James, he never did. But he needed to be.

He stared down at James who was wheezing as he dozed. Even in sleep, he kept trying to swallow, but he could not. His tongue had lesions on it and the few teeth he had left were too sensitive to chew with. His russet hair and beard were matted with dirt and sweat. He was exhausted from near permanent diarrhoea. His already small frame looked even more shrunken and twisted. He had already received absolution.

Buckingham listened out for his mother's footfalls. She was here in the palace, somewhere. They had to act quickly, the politics determined that. And now was the moment, before one of the doctors returned.

James had conceded far too much in his marriage negotiations with the French. This was partly because he was so ill, but mainly due to Richelieu's fiendishly clever reading of the man.

James Stuart loved one human being other than himself during the course of his idle and debauched life – his daughter Elizabeth. He had had high hopes for Henry, so did everybody, but he did not love him. Far from it, he resented his oldest son's precocious success.

So all Richelieu had to do was promise to help Elizabeth. Richelieu promised to send troops to the Palatinate to restore Elizabeth and Frederick to the throne. The cunning red eminence even mobilised French soldiers, sent them marching east then stopped them until James made concessions. But crucially the promise of help remained oral only. James's concessions to Richelieu were in writing, albeit in a document known as the Secret Letter. It was in the bureau drawer in James's bedroom.

Among the concessions James had made was the immediate cessation of all cases against Catholics for practising their religion, then complete freedom of religion in the future. Charles and Henrietta's children were to be brought up as Catholics until the age of ten.

This was impossible, Buckingham was completely sure of that. These guarantees violated the anti-Catholic promises both James and Charles had just made to Parliament. There would be roaring fire, revolt and revolution. It would consume combustible England.

But there was more, worse. According to the Secret Letter, Charles was to attend a marriage ceremony with Henrietta-Maria de Bourbon in Notre Dame Cathedral in Paris. It would be a Catholic ceremony, presided over by a Catholic archbishop. It would be seen as signalling for all the world Charles's conversion to Catholicism.

All those hours Buckingham had spent in boiling, airless Madrid, beating off impossible Spanish demands that Charles convert, and now Richelieu had achieved it in one cunning stroke. Charles's visit to Paris for the wedding must be stopped at all costs.

At first Buckingham thought that meant finding a way to halt the marriage, but England was already at war with Spain, using the privateers. They could ill-afford to have France at their throats, too. Then he realised the marriage was not the problem, the ceremony was. The marriage could go ahead, provided Charles was not at the ceremony. Proxies at weddings were not unusual.

Buckingham intended to nominate himself as proxy at the wedding. This would give him an excuse to go back to France with the casket of Anne of Austria's promise and finish what he had started that night at the Louvre, when he had danced with her.

And what could stop Charles going to France to attend his own wedding, to be replaced by a proxy? Only a cataclysmic event such as the death of James. James's extensive and prolonged period of dying had to end in death, and end now. The timing was all.

Where on earth was his mother? Buckingham strained his ears but still could not hear her coming.

Buckingham's mother, Mary Villiers, was one of the beauties of her age in her day and was still a fine-looking woman. She was like a great earthmother with her cub where her son George was concerned, providently hoarding the pennies on the modest estate in Goadby, Leicestershire; making sure her handsome son could dance, fence and ride with the best and crucially arranging his three-year stay in France where George became a man of the world.

George could tell her anything. She knew of his raging unslaked passion for Anne of Austria. She knew, approved and was ready to help. She would have been with him in the boudoir of seduction, if she could have managed it, cheering him on.

At that moment, Mary Villiers was in the spicery, run by Mr French. At a nod from her, Mr French threw her a complicit glance, left his fragrant world and busied himself elsewhere. Humming a Cardoso mass to herself, Mary Villiers ground some red cinnabar on a cold stone table. Some of it she mixed with syrup to form a paste, then bound it into a poultice. The rest of it she put ready to be added to a glass of strong wine.

When she was ready, she went off to join her son at James's bedside. There, she deftly applied the poultice under the dozing James's nightshirt, wrinkling her nose at the stench as she did so. Then her son forced the goblet of wine between James's lips. He woke up at that point, but Buckingham ignored his squeals of protest and pain as James had so often ignored his.

James's eyes opened wide. He held his arms out in supplication, struggling to sit up in bed. Then he gave a roar as the cinnabar began to do its work. It was a Sunday, the Lord's Day, and all around was still as James Stuart began his departure from this earth. He knew, at the last, he knew what was happening to him.

'Steenie, you dog,' he gasped out. 'You have done for me. You and that witch of a mother.'

Buckingham gave him a stare like glass. 'There is a poem by one Girolamo Fracastoro,' he ground out in a strange flat voice. 'It tells the story of a shepherd who for insulting Apollo was punished by an unknown pestilence. The pestilence brought out foul sores on his body. The shepherd's name was Syphilis.'

Buckingham took the Secret Letter from the bureau and threw it into the fire which blazed against the March cold. The French had their copy of course, but that could be denied or dismissed as a forgery.

James appeared to come back to life as the Secret Letter charred brown in the fire. He spluttered and gasped, the air rattling in his chest. Mary Villiers, ever enterprising, put a pillow over his face.

Later that day, Buckingham made a formal announcement to Charles that he was the new king: 'The news I bring is heavy on my tongue. The king your father is dead.'

Charles nodded thoughtfully, absently even. He asked what his father's last words had been. Buckingham quoted them, 'As I recall, His Majesty's last words upon this earth were Veni, Domine Jesu.'

Unlikely though this was, Charles affected to believe it.

A torchlight procession bore James's coffin to Denmark House, where his long-suffering queen, had once lived. Here it was to lie in state. The coffin was adorned with the eight silver candlesticks Charles had bought from Don Jerónimo Funes y Muñoz in Madrid.

The streets were thronged with apprentices and men of all trades, while the richer sort came to a halt as their carts and carriages choked the Strand, along with the new Hackney carriages, just coming into vogue.

After the lying in state, the mourners made their way to Westminster Abbey, where the Grand Cadazor, as James styled himself, the Great Huntsman, was to be laid to rest.

Charles had borrowed £50,000 on the Dutch money markets to fund the funeral. He wore long black robes and a black hood in simulation of sorrow. He was apprehensive about the future. Buckingham rode one place behind the coffin in his role as Master of the Horse.

The funeral oration was by John Williams, Bishop of Lincoln, chosen as someone sufficiently obscure and malleable to take up James's self-identification with Solomon as his theme. He developed this for some two hours. But the sermon also related to the catafalque, a superb creation by Inigo Jones which referenced James's apotheosis, his ascent into heaven.

The catafalque was an octagonal-faced, domed tempietto – a narrow egg-shaped dome, bigger than a man. As ever with Inigo, the design was derived from an earlier source, this time the catafalques of two Counter Reformation Popes. But – also as ever with Inigo – he had added his own genius and inspiration to the borrowing.

The catafalque reminded Charles of the dome of a cathedral. Below it were four statues identified by Bishop Williams as War, Peace, Religion and Justice. A steep set of stairs, inspired by Inigo's usual source, Palladio, led right up into the dome, which could be entered by mourners.

All was beauty for the death of the king.

# Chapter 14
## Notre Dame

The proxy marriage of Charles Stuart and Henrietta Maria de Bourbon could not take place within the hallowed portals of the Cathedral of Notre Dame because Charles was a Protestant. Instead, it took place on a specially erected wedding stage outside the west door.

The floor of the stage was spread with purple velvet embroidered with gold fleur-de-lys. The walls were draped with rich tapestries, some of them sent from the Mortlake tapestry works. A huge gold awning arching over the assembled dignitaries was intended to give protection from the sun, but from early morning a spring rain, cold for May, had poured in streams. This was held to be a bad omen.

A specially constructed wooden walkway led from the stage to rooms in the Archbishop's Palace, where the newly wedded couple would have consummated their marriage, at least symbolically, before a large audience. This clearly could not happen in the absence of the groom.

The French were furious at Buckingham's last-minute fait accompli of a proxy wedding, but they had little choice but to accept it. A noted pro-Anglican, the Duc de Chevreuse, played the part of Charles in his ceremonial role. Chevreuse was dressed in black because Charles was still in mourning for his father, which at least was a convincing reason for his absence. But in keeping with the glory of the occasion his black cloak was encrusted with gold and diamonds.

As to the now sixteen-year-old bride, she was in love. She had been in love with her soon-to-be husband ever since she had first set eyes on him that evening when she had danced for him – and only him – at the Louvre Palace.

And then, as part of the extensive and tedious marriage negotiations, a diplomat acting for the English, a pretty little fellow called Wat Montagu, had given her a miniature of Charles to keep. The miniature, Wat Montagu explained in his excellent French, was by Peter Oliver. Painted in the year of Charles and Henrietta's first meeting, 1623, it was a watercolour on vellum of great delicacy and beauty.

Henrietta could not believe her good fortune that the beardless beautiful boy in this painting was to be her husband. Above the stiff ruff she saw a noble and sensitive face, with a high forehead betokening intelligence. The scraps of moustache made him look younger, and so closer to her age, than he actually was. She knew he was twenty-five, but that was surely ideal. Henrietta had a chain made so the miniature could hang between her breasts in a cornelian case made to protect it.

As the wedding vows were solemnly uttered between Henrietta and the stand-in for her husband, the far part of the stage collapsed. There was a gasp then a groan from the attendees and bystanders, not in fear of injury but horror at such a bad omen.

As Henrietta watched, fascinated, the painter Rubens was thrown to the ground, all sprawling lost dignity. Henrietta gave her bell-like laugh. What fun! If only that pompous dandy Buckingham had been here to end up in a heap, like the painter. She had suffered his preening arrogance during the negotiations and vastly preferred Wat Montagu.

But Buckingham had missed the proxy wedding. He had been delayed by extensive wrangles with Parliament, who as usual were not granting His Majesty the money he needed to rule. Arriving after the ceremony, he had visited his old haunts in Paris, from where he sent an outrageous note to Richelieu saying he had no time to meet him but enquired about buying the Mona Lisa from the French

Royal collection. He was delighted with himself for having tweaked Richelieu's beard.

Before he left, he had arranged a commemorative medal of the great event. It was a pendant portrait of king and queen shown under rays from heaven. The reverse showed Cupid scattering roses and lilies. The medals were by Nicolas Briot, the gold and silversmith. They were a signal to joy among the people, a source of happiness.

Henrietta had one of the commemorative medals, a gift from the pretty elf, as she thought of Mr Montagu. It joined the miniature of Charles in her bosom where it stayed throughout the ceremony.

The dandy Buckingham was due shortly, as usual very much at his own convenience. Henrietta and her retinue were to set off for England, with Buckingham as the new queen's personal escort.

Henrietta had no expectations past this point in her life. It was a blank, a void. Her ignorance of England was so total, her lively imagination had no first foothold to grip with. She spoke not a single word of English. She knew nothing of the people and their history and little of their culture.

She knew they were Protestants. She had had to promise the Pope, Urban VIII, that she would do her best for the Catholics over there. But then Urban VIII was her godfather, so to accede to his wishes was only polite. Exactly how she was to further Catholicism in England was of no interest to her. Indeed, the thought provoked one of those massive yawns she gave in public occasionally, when protocol became too much.

England? What was England? She would be queen of what, exactly? And she was already uneasy about Buckingham and the power he wielded.

# CHAPTER 15
## PETER-PAUL RUBENS

York House, Buckingham's pile in the Strand, was made in his own image. It embodied his shrewd dealings. The house was owned by the Archbishopric of York, though no Archbishop of York had actually lived in it since Mary's time. The dilapidated property was traditionally leased to the Lord Chancellor of the day for a peppercorn rent of £11 a year.

Buckingham had expertly eased out the incumbent Lord Chancellor, Nicholas Bacon, the philosopher Francis Bacon's father. The philosopher himself was then quickly prevailed on to sell Buckingham the lease outright for £1,300. It said everything about Buckingham's dealings with his fellow man that Bacon was delighted with the transaction, valuing the goodwill of the King's favourite above profit and property.

Once installed, Buckingham set about extensive renovation in the Palladian style. This featured the creation of a handsome crenelated central block flanked by two pedimented wings. Passers-by in the Strand, the artistic heart of London, would be struck by the tall windows above a loggia in this imposing main block.

So York House was a worthy home to one of the finest art collections in England, soon to be the finest in the world, when Buckingham had exercised his considerable will. It would eclipse, in particular, the collection of Thomas Howard, Lord Arundel, the only man in England with the temerity to rival him, Buckingham, as collector and connoisseur.

The collection already boasted more than twenty Titians, who Buckingham revered as much as Charles did, certainly since he had seen Titian's *Charles V on Horseback* at the Escorial, and perhaps before. One of the Titians was the *Portrait of a Secretary*. Visiting York House, Inigo Jones had sunk to his knees, tears streaming down his gnarled face at the sight of it.

There were also sixteen works by Veronese, two by Correggio and a Giorgione. And there were some Caravaggios, that prince of darkness who had so mastered light. Caravaggio's deep darkness and jets of bright light mirrored something in Buckingham, who was nothing if not a man of extremes.

And there was the Velazquez portrait of Charles, painted in Madrid, hanging in the Long Gallery at York House. Charles did not want this reminder of his infatuation with the Infanta to hang in Whitehall just as her successor in his affections arrived from France.

Charles was also uneasy about Buckingham's planned meeting with Rubens in Paris, though he accepted the necessity of it. Rubens was a well-paid agent of the Spanish government, as such he influenced any possible return of Elizabeth and Frederick to their lands. Buckingham's view was the more they could draw Rubens in as an artist and a dealer, the greater the sway they would have over him politically.

Buckingham had art dealings as well as commissions planned with Rubens. Then, when he was ready, he would set about escorting Henrietta back to her new kingdom. His agents had told him that Anne of Austria was at Amiens, which conveniently lay on their route from Paris to Boulogne, where they would take ship to England. Buckingham had brought with him the casket she had given him at the Louvre, the sign of Anne's acceptance of him, or at least of his pursuit. Rubens had painted Anne of Austria; that was an omen.

It was typical of Buckingham that he did not find this programme of dealing, escorting and seduction especially onerous or daunting and had no doubt whatsoever of his success on all fronts.

In dealings with men, Buckingham favoured the principle of the Big Promise. His adversary must be offered the hope of large gain. In dealings with women, Buckingham regarded his own fair form as the large gain. He was in no doubt of the big promise to Rubens, agreed in advance with Charles.

Some six years ago, a furious fire had consumed the Banqueting House at Whitehall. The carpenters had left a taper glowing when they were working on the scenery for a masque. It was a terrible time for both Charles and Buckingham. Samuel Daniel, author of Tethys Festival, died a couple of months later, quickly followed by Charles's mother, who Buckingham was fond of.

However, Inigo Jones, the *uomo universale* Surveyor of Works, had created a masterpiece as his new Banqueting House. In Buckingham's view he was a far greater architect than Robert Strickells, who designed the original. Now, Rubens was to be commissioned to paint a huge ceiling of nine panels for the new Banqueting House. Like the funeral catafalque, the ceiling was to show the apotheosis of James Stuart, his ascent to heaven.

A gleam came into Rubens's eye as Buckingham dangled the commission, a gleam Buckingham knew well, part worldly ambition part artistic fulfilment. They were speaking in a studio in the Louvre. Louis had made it available to Rubens for as long as he needed it, after the proxy wedding.

Buckingham threw him an appraising glance. Rubens was fifteen years older than him. He was still handsome at forty-eight. He was widely read and ferociously clever. Buckingham suppressed an uncharacteristic flash of jealousy at the blessings God had showered on the painter. Peter-Paul Rubens was a naturally happy man, and Buckingham was anything but that.

Born in obscurity in Siegen in Westphalia, apparent misfortunes had turned out to be no such thing, as fate washed him and his mother into Antwerp in the Spanish Netherlands and made him a Catholic. It was the perfect place and the perfect circumstances for an artist.

In Antwerp, he was apprenticed to two ploddingly competent masters, Tobias Verhaecht, a painter of unremarkable but saleable landscapes and Otto van Veen. Van Veen was a Romanist who had studied in Italy, so he liked to call himself Vaunius. Rubens learned to paint by paying lip service to them and copying Holbein.

He was aided by prodigious talent, though untouched by genius. His recent self-portrait, in Buckingham's view, showed only an elegant, full-bearded man with a long face in a broad hat. It conveyed authority and repose. It showed nothing of the soul of the man. It did not breathe.

Nevertheless, Rubens was one of the leading painters in Europe. As a man, he was emollient, charming, smooth and fluent. He was also basically decent. Endymion Porter had known him for years, right back to his boyhood as a page to the Olivares family. Endymion always vouched for him.

With all these attributes, Rubens was born for the diplomatic service, becoming a key agent for Spain. The diplomatic world and the world of art dealing were inextricably intertwined. To be a practising painter was a further advantage. Rubens slid easily and gracefully into his world, like slipping into warm water, then glided around within it, like a fish.

On this, their first afternoon together, Buckingham arranged to buy Rubens's whole cabinet of art works for 100,000 florins. This included thirteen pictures by Rubens himself, along with other paintings, statues and medals. Buckingham was pleased with his acquisitions, but never lost sight of the tactical dimension. He would tell Charles there may be some benefit for Elizabeth and Frederick, one day.

He then, with some well-concealed inner excitement, agreed a fee of a hefty £500 for a full-length equestrian portrait of himself. He wished to be heroicised, indeed immortalised.

The commission was fortuitously timed: Rubens, always prodigious in output, had just delivered the last fifteen of a series of twenty-four paintings for the Luxembourg Palace. He was now pinned in Paris, laid up because a shoemaker had badly wrenched his foot while fitting a new pair of boots.

Rubens smilingly made light of the foot problem, limping to his canvas to make an immediate start on the commission with some preliminary sketches. In a letter to his wife, he later made clear his opinion of Buckingham – 'capricious and arrogant' – though none of that showed through the practised diplomatic mask as he worked. Neither did the shrewdness of his assessment of his sitter's fate: 'He seems to me forced by his own daring either to triumph or to die gloriously.'

Rubens was always happy to talk as he worked. They dropped easily into Spanish court gossip about Olivares and the king, then movements in the Madrid art market, then on to a crisp, frank summary of official Spanish policy about Charles's marriage to Henrietta, an alliance which the Spanish naturally opposed. Rubens then assured Buckingham of the Spanish desire for peace with England and its privateers which he, Rubens, was about to negotiate on their behalf in London.

Buckingham was interested and entertained, Rubens made sure of that. While still smoothly speaking – almost inevitably he had a glorious voice, sapid as wine – he had pinned a piece of paper onto the easel and taken some black and some white chalk. He started to wave both arms, as if conducting himself speaking. The chalk made the faintest of contact with the paper.

After a while, Rubens fell silent. Buckingham, fascinated, silently watched the painter's movements. The faint scrapes of chalk on paper were the only sounds in the room.

Eventually, Rubens indicated with an imperious nod of the head that he was finished. He waved Buckingham to him. Buckingham, humbled before art as he had never been before man or woman, trotted across the studio to the easel like a child or a servant.

And what a wonder he beheld. The sketch showed his face daringly close up. It peered into the orifices of eyes, nose, mouth, into the very essence. One or two lines gave context and the whole face was framed by a fiery halo of tangled auburn hair. The power was there, as well as the beauty. Gazing slightly to his left through luminous eyes below elegantly arched eyebrows the man in this sketch could have bidden the world to his will. Anne of Austria, surely, would have succumbed on the spot if she beheld it.

That indeed was Buckingham's thought. It made him bellow with laughter. He clapped Rubens hard on the shoulder, asserting himself again. He bowed before art not the artist.

'Fine work, Rubens. Fine work.'

They discussed how Buckingham wished to be portrayed in his equestrian full-length portrait. Buckingham had purchased the role of Admiral of the Fleet from Charles Howard, Duke of Nottingham for a price which included a £3,000 pension for life for Howard.

Admiral of the Fleet was a key role for a power that did all its fighting by sea. He instructed that he be portrayed in this role. The theme would no doubt involve Neptune, God of the Sea.

Rubens always worked quickly. Buckingham posed for the portrait in the Louvre for eight days, which was about the length of time he had expected. The eight days ushered in a deep and lasting disappointment with Rubens' work.

Looking back on it, Buckingham felt he should not have been surprised. Rubens had an exquisite touch with drawings; his drawings of the faces of young children were delicate masterpieces of tenderness and love. But working on the massive scale he loved so much, the bombast dominated; the mask of the diplomat fell between creator and viewer and what was left was empty and as often as not clumsy.

Buckingham needed all his own diplomatic skills when he saw the first version of the equestrian portrait. The horse was fine; Rubens was good at horses. It was a chestnut and reared up, as they did, so Buckingham could show his mastery of it. The fleet was in the distance under the horse's belly, so Buckingham was controlling that, too. Fine!

But Buckingham himself looked scarcely out of boyhood and wore an expression of slightly startled surprise. The French or Spanish might be tempted to give this Admiral of the Fleet a square meal and send him home, if they captured him. They certainly would have no fear of him. And the naiad bringing gifts of the sea to the feared ruler was nearly as big as he was.

A second version, politely if a little coolly requested, saw the mounted Buckingham more central, while a fuller beard at least confirmed that he had reached manhood. Nevertheless, Buckingham requested a larger painting with more allegorical devices to his glory. This, it was agreed, should be a victory goddess with a laurel wreath in her right hand and a cornucopia in her left and a wind god. Buckingham also asked for a second goddess subduing discord, as often played out in masques

The armada of warships, Buckingham also stipulated, should be made more imposing. 'Enough to frighten the Spanish.'

Rubens smiled, before readily and uncomplainingly agreeing to any further changes Buckingham wished to make, no matter how many versions of the picture that required. In the end there were five.

At this point, Buckingham showed his feeling for composition by suggesting he should be controlling his rearing horse right-centre of the picture, rather than plumb in the middle. This was instinct on Buckingham's part, he did not know himself why he had requested it. But the result, coupled with an increase to the size of the duke relative to the horse, resulted in a sense of forward motion.

Finally, the piece could be said to move, even if it could not be said to live.

# CHAPTER 16
## THE TOKEN

When he left for Paris, Buckingham had taken with him twenty-seven suits. His favourite among them was of white velvet trimmed with diamonds which was rumoured to be worth more than the entire exchequer, over eighty thousand pounds. Buckingham liked to wear it with a hat jewel studded with pearls and diamonds which the royal jewellers, the Duarte family, had purchased for him in the Netherlands for 150,000 guilders.

The hat jewel was in the shape of an anchor. Buckingham had first worn it when he purchased the title of Admiral of the Fleet. He made a point of wearing this showy Admiral of the Fleet insignia on his first official visit to the French court, soon after the proxy wedding, to rub French noses in the threat of English sea power.

He then adorned himself with every diamond he had brought with him for his next visit to the French court, so diamonds sparkled from his sword, his girdle, his hatband and a feather in his cap entirely encrusted with diamonds. The French dubbed him *cet étranger présomptueux*.

When the presumptuous stranger finally departed from Paris, along with Henrietta and her attendants and retinue, he did not travel with them but in the three coaches he had brought with him, each lined with velvet and gold lace.

The travelling party was to stop in Amiens so Henrietta could visit her mother there. This suited Buckingham perfectly, giving him enough time and opportunity to present the casket and take Anne of Austria to his bed.

Henrietta's loathing for Buckingham had only increased on the journey to Amiens. She was among a minority of women who did not find him especially desirable. Now her fists clenched at the very thought of him.

At Amiens, Buckingham was wearing a suit of purple satin embroidered from head to foot with orient pearls and a dashing Spanish-style cloak. Anne, meanwhile, still felt neglected by her pious and serious-minded husband. Louis, she felt, neglected her emotionally, intellectually and in the bed chamber. She also felt he despised her for being unable to give him an heir. Her failure, as she was made to see it, saw her weep bitter tears of frustration and hurt.

Louis had been proud that Hugo Grotius had dedicated his *De Jure Belli et Pacis* to him. He did not stop talking about it. Anne wanted embraces, passion and some decent conversation and to hell with *De Jure Belli et Pacis*.

Her bitterness with her husband was compounded when Louis sent her Spanish entourage back to the Madrid court, completing her isolation, leaving her barely able to communicate in her broken French.

When she heard Buckingham was approaching Amiens, she was excited. She invited him to her levée, a public court carried out as the monarch dressed in the bedroom. Anne had so organised matters that by the time Buckingham was shown into the levée, the only other person present was the ancient Comtesse de Lannoi, her most trusted attendant.

Anne had arranged herself carefully in bed. Buckingham threw himself on his knees, took out the casket she had given him that evening two years ago and declared it was either love or death for him and that his fate lay in her hands. He kissed the coverlet of her bed in transports of passion.

Anne sent the Comtesse de Lannoi away, smilingly indicated that she did not wish to be responsible for the death of so beauteous a man and drew back the coverlet, letting him in. Later she received him in public in front of the whole court at Amiens, allowing him to kneel at her feet and kiss her hand.

## CHAPTER 17
## CAST OUT OF PARADISE

Princess Henrietta-Maria de Bourbon was raised in paradise, at least that is how it felt to her at the time. This was not at the Louvre, a palace she hardly knew, but at St Germain-en-Laye. Earthbound mortals believed St Germain-en-Laye to be a two-hour carriage ride from Paris. But ethereal beings like Henrietta-Maria de Bourbon knew where it really was. It was on a star at the peak of the heavens, entered only by those in a state of bliss.

Even in mundane reality, the little palace was lovely enough. It was a brick and stone Renaissance style chateau perched on a wooded hill overlooking the Seine. Endless lovely gardens fronted it, with grottos and fountains and exquisite sculptures by the magical hand of Hubert le Sueur.

There was one grotto where a fountain of seashells and coral played. It was her secret place. A griffon spouted water and by clever mechanics a sculptured nightingale was made to sing by weight of water. So the ear was pleased as well as the other senses.

These mechanics – there was another of Neptune spouting water – were the work of an Italian master, Tomaso Francini, who also laid out the shaded walks, trellised roses and avenues of fruit trees in the formal gardens which stepped their way all the way down to the Seine.

And frolicking in the palace and playing in the gardens was the *troupeau* – the little flock. The little flock was the ten children of Henri IV of France, five of them, like Henrietta, born in wedlock and the other five outside it. Not that Henrietta was aware of any differences or distinctions as they played.

The children staged entertainments for their parents and for the courtiers. There were ballets and comedies with elaborate costumes and sets. As soon as she could walk, Henrietta remembered dressing up, singing, dancing, then running wild through the countryside.

What supervision there was, was provided by the governess, a benign mother-hen officially entitled Madame de Montglat but known to the children as Mamangat. Mamangat was important to Henrietta but not as important as her daughter, Jeanne de St Georges, known as Mamie – which meant *mon amie.*

Henrietta thought she and Mamie were shaped from the same soul. Like Henrietta, poor Mamie had no father, he had died when she was little, as Henri IV had. So Henrietta saw herself as Mamie's protector, as well as her friend.

Of the others in the *troupeau* Henrietta was most distant from her older brother, Louis. He left the *troupeau-*paradise at the age of eight to become Louis XIII, king of France. But he was a cold fish anyway, even as a boy.

Henrietta could talk, dance and frolic easily with her sister Christine, who, being younger, gave Henrietta the chance of being older, which she enjoyed immensely. But of the siblings she was closest to her brother Gaston, known always, even in her thoughts, as 'dear Gaston'.

They were as close in age as siblings could be. They looked alike, too, though Gaston lacked Henrietta's sharp intelligence which shone through her bright eyes. Henrietta told everybody that she and Gaston were really twins, it was just that she had politely given him a few months start in life because she did not wish to leave her mother's womb, any more than she ever wished to leave the little palace at St Germain-en-Laye.

Adults played along with the twins idea. Henrietta and Gaston were christened together by Cardinal de Bonzi. More significantly to Henrietta, they were often dressed alike in white satin suits for formal occasions, sometimes even for plays.

When they were not putting on plays, playing music, singing or dancing she and Gaston used to run through the wild woods and end up playing *joucheries* out of doors. It was a game similar to spellicans, a pick-up-sticks game played with *jouchets*, small sticks they carved from rushes. Henrietta and Gaston took the game very seriously, the one who picked up the most sticks without disturbing the pile being entitled to all sorts of privileges until they played next time. Henrietta usually won.

When she played with Gaston, or with the other boys, or when she ran through woods or splashed through streams alone, it seemed obvious to her to wear Gaston's clothes not her own.

How could she run free with all those bulging petticoats? Not to mention the farthingales. They tried to make even little girls wear them. What freedom could there be wearing a cage round your legs? Henrietta enlisted the willing help of Mamie and Mamengat to wear Gaston's breeches, boots and jerkin the whole time.

There was some schooling at the *troupeau*, though not very much. There were sporadic and far from compulsory sessions with an orientalist called Francois Savary. Henrietta's instruction with M Savary did not include any foreign languages or the study of maps, a lack she first noticed at the age of fifteen when told she was to become queen of England.

The formal instruction she enjoyed most was the dance – coranto, galliard, bourrée, branle and saraband. She mastered them all and delighted in doing so. She also had some training for her naturally excellent singing voice.

And when all that singing and dancing and running around made her hungry, there was ample good food, always important to the Bourbon family. Oh, the egg soup with lemon juice! And the cock's combs. The chicken roasted and fried in breadcrumbs. The mutton, veal and pork.

They were near the coast, so oysters were brought in barrels of seawater. And oh! fruit tarts and comfits made with all the spices under the sun. Not to mention cheese from nearby Brie. Henrietta had drunk wine with a little water in it for as long as she could remember. It made her heady with joy, sending the magic world spinning round her.

Then the world stopped spinning and went grey. She was a princess. Princesses were sent away to marry princes. At the age of sixteen she was to be sent to England to marry a prince by the name of Charles Stuart.

'Gaston,' she told her elective twin, 'I don't want to go.'

Gaston had promised to accompany her until she was out of sight of France. He rode with her in the royal coach. At Henrietta's insistence so did Mamie, now appointed her chief Lady in Waiting.

All the way to Amiens the skies were a cerulean blue, befitting a June day in France. But then, as if the sun itself were saying goodbye to turn back the way it had come, low cloud covered the skies. Henrietta had never been close to her mother, Marie de Medici, the clouded farewells were terse and formal.

However, after Amiens a change came over Buckingham. He was farouche and wild-eyed. All restraint gone he charged around giving unwanted information about journey timings and assuring Henrietta endlessly how much Charles was looking forward to meeting her. Henrietta met his gaze with a blank stare.

By the time they reached Boulogne a north-westerly storm had started up. Their first sight of the ship which would carry her away, *The Prince*, was at sheet anchor. Henrietta was more interested in the sea than the ship. She had never seen the sea before.

Next day, a Sunday, the storm had eased leaving the sky sulky, the sun still absent. Gaston offered to take Henrietta out in a rowing boat to familiarise her with the strange salty substance which would bear her away. Henrietta's smile as she accepted the offer was the first Gaston had seen from her in months. So out they went in what was known as Boulogne Road where the ships were anchored, Gaston rowing mightily.

'Dip your fingers in it,' he shouted to her.

She threw her head back, laughed and did as he said. Then she licked her fingers.

'Bah!'

'Oh, you little fool, Hen-Hen!'

For the journey, Henrietta had chosen a colourful silk *déshabillés* embellished with gold silver and lace. It had puff sleeves – *manche serrée de peluche* – that she thought becoming. But before she could have her luggage stowed in her cabin, Buckingham had to finish organising the retinue.

Apart from Mamie, the only attendant in her retinue Henrietta had chosen herself was the sculptor, Hubert le Sueur. Le Sueur had already designed the figures on the frieze for James's catafalque. The commission had come from Inigo Jones, who was impressed by his work. Henrietta was delighted at this honour to her favourite sculptor and insisted on bringing him with her, to an appointment at Charles's court.

Le Sueur was a Huguenot, a French Protestant. This interested Henrietta considerably less than the beauty of his sculptures. She already longed for his statue of Diana back in a grotto at St Germain-en-Laye. But she apprehended with dawning strength and sadness that her indifference to religion would not be allowed to last.

Her retinue had been chosen by Cardinal Richelieu. It was massive. She was bringing a complete court from counts and countesses to cooks and maids. She had her own treasurer, physician, surgeon and apothecary. There were cupbearers and carvers, wardrobe keepers and valets. All presided over by the French Ambassador, de Tillières.

Henrietta understood all too well, even at the age of sixteen, that no foreign court could swallow another court whole like this. But even that was not the worst of it. Just about all Henrietta knew of England was that it was a Protestant country. She was bringing twenty-eight Catholic priests, a bishop, two abbots, chaplains and twelve Oratorian priests headed by the founder of their order, Father Pierre Bérulle, who would be her confessor.

The Oratorians were to serve mass in the Queen's chapel. Being loaded on board *The Prince* and a flotilla of sister ships were gold and silver crosses for the altars, gold and silver chalices for the holy wine and pyxes and monstrances for consecrated bread. There were sets of vestments and altar cloths. There were holy books with the lives of the saints and works to convert the English unbelievers, who did not want any of this.

But worst of all, this army of religion was headed by Bishop Mendy, who was Richelieu's nephew. He was there as Richelieu's eyes in England, a spy in fact. And surely anything Henrietta confessed to Father Bérulle would be reported directly back to the Cardinal too.

Henrietta feared the English would take one look at her and see only a Catholic troublemaker. They would know that Pope Urban had made her promise to be the Esther, Clothilde and Aldiberga of her people. She knew who Esther was, at least, but had never heard of Clothilde or Aldiberga. Not that that would not stop the English hating her on sight.

She wept in Mamie's arms before the ship had even left Boulogne.

Some ten hours later Henrietta was beyond tears. She was pacing a tiny antechamber in Dover Castle with her small fists clenched, eyes narrowed to black points of fury. Outside, the sky was the lowest and blackest she had ever seen. Rain was pouring down, streaming in runnels down the ancient battlements.

'How dare they! How dare they! I am a Bourbon princess. They shall not dishonour me so lightly.'

'Wait, my dear.' Mamie was wailing in her despair at ever bringing comfort. 'There will be a reason. Give them a chance.'

'Huh!'

Almost as soon as they had left Boulogne harbour a massive storm blew up. Henrietta was sick all over her beautiful travelling dress, the dress she had hoped to wear for Charles. She had now changed into another one, with Mamie's help, but the change of plan had upset her.

When they finally arrived in this new kingdom of hers she was thrown into prison. At least that was how the massively mouldering Dover Castle appeared to her. It was very much a fortress not a palace.

Brought up in the dainty St Germaine-en-Laye with occasional trips to glorious Fontainebleau, which her own saint of a father had largely rebuilt, or to the imposing majesty of the Louvre, she had seen nothing like this dilapidated Dover Castle before and did not wish to see anything like it again.

Most of the French party had been quartered in the town, or the surrounding countryside, she had no idea where they were, actually. She and Mamie had been led up unspeakably filthy curving stone steps inside the fortress and allocated a suite of dingy rooms with furniture fit only for firewood.

And there they were abandoned. There was no sign whatsoever of the prince who was now her husband. Buckingham, having completed his duty by bringing her this far, disappeared, presumably to London, with no explanation. One of his followers, a huge man by the name of Endymion Porter, explained in excellent French that Charles had been at Dover Castle in good time to greet her, but he had now left.

Henrietta screamed 'Left! Left! Where has he gone?'

Endymion bowed deeply. 'I believe that His Majesty was called away to Canterbury. But he is even now returning and should be here shortly.'

Henrietta screamed again.

At that moment they heard a commotion from down the stairs to the rooms below. Charles Stuart had arrived.

# CHAPTER 18
## *BLISS!*

Charles stumbled into the room, tilted forward on tiptoe. His rickets condition had eased with age and the sun in Spain, but his body was still twisted slightly to the left and he was uncomfortable with his heels down.

Endymion gave him a warm smile and went to stand outside the room. After a glance from Henrietta, Mamie went with him. Charles and Henrietta were alone in a shabby anteroom in Dover Castle.

He glanced at her, then blew his cheeks out with relief. She was shorter than him. Then he noticed her lustrous eyes, sparkling like stars, gaze fixed on his face. There was a flash of pearly little teeth, his main memory of her from that night in the Louvre. He opened his mouth to say something (What? He had no idea) when to his astonishment she dropped to her knees.

Henrietta had rehearsed this little speech back in France, with Gaston playing the part of Charles. It had left them convulsed with giggles, 'Sire, je suis venue en ce pays pour votre majesté pour estre usée et commandée de vous.' (Sire, I have come to this country to be used and commanded by you.) She added that a woman should have no will other than that of her husband.

Charles stared at her. Her head was lowered so he could see only the top of her dark, auburn-streaked hair. For a moment there was complete silence. Then Charles smiled. Her shoulders were shaking. Princess Henrietta-Maria de Bourbon was laughing like a waterspout.

Charles had been refreshing his knowledge of French. He enjoyed learning foreign languages. He had learned some Spanish before the trip to Madrid with Buckingham but had no opportunity to use it. In preparation for Henrietta's arrival he had re-read much of the considerable correspondence he and Henry had had with the French court and even with artists like Rubens, who always wrote in French. When he spoke, the language came easily to him.

'Marriage is the queen of friendships,' he said. He had prepared the quotation. It had been supplied by his chaplain, Jeremy Taylor. 'You have not fallen into the hands of strangers, my dear.'

He was about to say something else when she rose gracefully to her feet and berated him.

'Where have you been?' Her voice was rising high. 'We have been waiting for you. They said you were here. They said you had gone. Where did you go? What is more important than your princess?' She stared at him. 'Oh! You look sad. Has something bad happened?'

'Ye… ye… yes. I'm afraid it has. I have just had word that a great man has died.'

'No!' Her eyes were pools of wonder.

'Mmm yes. His name was Orlando Gibbons. He died at Canterbury. That is where I went.'

'Orlando Gibbons, the great musician? You *know* Orlando Gibbons?'

'Oh yes. I used to dance to his music when I was a child, with my sister. Then later he was a friend. A man with a fine soul. You see, I play in a violin and viol ensemble, called Coperario's Musique. Orlando played with us from time to time, on the harpsichord. He played at my father's funeral. It was the last time I saw him in good health.'

'But that is wonderful, Charles. You play music? You love music?'

'Oh yes, yes. Giovanni Coperario himself taught me the viol. Nicholas Lanier, our Master of Music, tells me I am quite a skilful player,' Charles pouted.

Henrietta clapped her hands together. 'I play the lute. I love music. We must play together, husband and wife making music.'

'I should like that very much. There are pieces by Orlando we could play. Do you know "See, see the world is incarnate."?'

'Yes, yes. We know his work in France. A piece for the virginals was sent to us transcribed as sheet music, the first ever in the whole wide world I heard it said.'

Charles clasped his hands together in front of his body, unconsciously imitating her earlier feminine gesture.

'Henrietta, that piece for the virginals was played at my sister's wedding to Frederick.'

Tears came to Charles's eyes at the memory of the promise of that time, before the loss of that wretched battle outside Prague had brought it all crashing down.

'Oh Charles. How sad. How sad. She is in Holland now, is she not?' Henrietta suddenly sounded mature, for the first time more woman than girl.

'Yes. That's right.'

'Gaston told me all about it. My brother, that is. Oh, you must love her so much.'

He smiled. 'I do.'

'But let us talk of happy things. We have someone in common, you know? You and I. He is from our households. A servant. Can you guess who it is?' Now the woman was gone again and the girl was back, impish, teasing.

Charles felt his smile growing wider and wider. 'I have no idea.'

'Do you want me to tell you?' She twinkled like a mischievous pixie.

'Please do,' he said, solemnly.

'It is... M de St Antoine!'

'Of course! The riding master.'

'My *father's* riding master. My papa sent him to the English court out of love. But he came back home sometimes to visit us. He taught me and Gaston to ride.'

'Oh, Henrietta! This is... is... is. I feel God must have sent you to me. Such a bond. Do you know, before you came I was reading some of my dear dead brother Henry's letters to your father. Your father was Henry's godfather.'

'No! I never knew. But then I was so young when...'

Charles remembered she was nine years younger than him. 'Your father was a second father to Henry.'

'Tell me! Tell me!'

'We hoped your father would join a Protestant alliance with Frederick. He was...'

'Yes, he became a Huguenot. If my mother can marry a Protestant so can I.'

Charles shook with laughter at that, both hands holding his protruding hips. 'I remember your father sending Henry armour, pistols and a sword as well as M de St Antoine, his own riding instructor. I was reading Henry's letter of thanks to your father just the other day.'

'It is wonderful, these bonds between us. And, you know, it is wonderful that we met over dance. That you saw me dancing, with gay music playing and the beauty of a masque.'

'Yes. It is wonderful. And so are you.'

Then they were kissing, he diffidently, she with surprising force; kissing with open tongue.

When Charles had just arrived back from Canterbury, just before he went up to Henrietta, Endymion had murmured in his ear that the room he had used before setting sail for Madrid had again been made ready for him. He wanted to spare Charles the public lying-together ceremony. He knew Charles hated the thought of it.

Charles took Henrietta by the hand and led her up a flight of stone stairs to the next level. Henrietta looked round for Mamie, but Endymion had thought of everything – the loyal M St Georges was at that moment tucking into a plate of bread, ham and cheese washed down by a flagon of small beer in the kitchen.

144

Once alone in the bedroom, Henrietta again surprised Charles with her passion. Neither of them had done this before. Both were rather hazy about the details. Henrietta was wearing a dress identical to the one soiled on the voyage, but in green not red. Charles had on a blue satin doublet and hose.

Charles nearly stopped altogether when he lifted her petticoats as they were so lovely frothily white and so beautifully embroidered. But her angry grunts led him to continue. The big surprise was the blood when he penetrated her. Neither of them knew quite what to do but she instinctively reassured him.

'C'est sans importance.' Mamie's mother, Mamangat, had warned her it might hurt the first time and she assumed the blood was something to do with the hurting.

But after the hurt she dissolved into him with all her being. He felt passionate pleasure and love at her. It went on for much longer than she had expected, the pleasure becoming so intense she briefly fainted into his arms.

Finally, at the age of twenty-five, Charles Stuart had found something he was good at. Outside, it finally stopped raining.

# CHAPTER 19
## THE NEW KINGDOM

The royal couple entered London by water. They were rowed along the Thames upriver in the royal barge, as rain fell relentlessly. A bad omen? If it was, it was ignored. Hundreds of small boats followed the state barge. Warships decked out in bunting fired off their guns in honour. Celebratory fireworks exploded in the sky, defying the rain to dampen them.

Cheering crowds thronged both banks of the river. Henrietta, they thought, was beautiful and sweet natured. She and Charles stood by the barge's open windows and waved to them through the rain. They were dressed in matching green to show their oneness and the new life of spring – fertility.

England's young soon-to-be crowned king had married his princess. It was a relief from the misery of the plague which had already cut swathes through the people. It was a relief from the relentless grind of daily life. It was a new fresh wind blowing away the fetid stench of James's reign.

On the royal couple sailed, bearers of hope, under London Bridge, on past the City, on past St Paul's Cathedral, awaiting renovation, then parallel to the Strand, its mansions home to courtiers like Buckingham, artists like Rubens when he was in London, physicians like Theodore Mayerne and prosperous merchants who wished to be near the artists.

Henrietta admired the ordered, well-planned gardens of the mansions on the Strand as they led down in steppes to the northern bank of the Thames. It reminded her of St Germain-en-Laye and the exquisite gardens and artefacts of Tomaso Francini.

The royal barge cast anchor at Whitehall Privy Stairs. To cheers from the throng, Henrietta beheld Whitehall Palace.

'What on earth is this? Where are we, Charles?'

'Whitehall Palace, dear heart. Your new home.'

Henrietta looked around her. 'Yes, but where is the palace?' She turned 360 degrees, pointy little steps. 'This is a village. Where is the palace?'

Charles laughed. He had been working hard on the plans for the new Whitehall Palace and poring over elevations of what was there now. He knew precisely that the hodgepodge of random mouldering Tudor buildings Henrietta was staring at in horror contained no fewer than 53 buildings with 1,400 chambers, most of them interconnected, all of them in disrepair.

Henrietta screamed. 'What is that?'

'What?' Charles was alarmed.

'There is a road right through the middle of this village you call a palace. Look! Carts! Peasants! There is a peasant driving sheep! In the middle of the palace!'

Charles pouted indulgently. 'Yes, that is King Street. It runs through the palace buildings. When I build the new palace I will move all that area down to the riverside and build my glorious new palace in St James's Park. You will marvel at it, Henrietta. Inigo and I have planned eleven new courtyards and a chapel as big as a cathedral. It will be a riverside palace to rival Charles V's at the Alhambra in Granada, which Inigo has studied.'

She was half-listening. She seized his arm. 'There is a market in the middle of your palace.'

'Well, not a mar... market exactly. They are allowed to put up stalls along the outside of the palace walls. They sell food mostly. We licence them but most of them are unlicensed, at the moment. Must see about that.'

'Huh!'

'Over there...' Charles pointed through the rain '... there are the tennis courts, the bowling alley and the cockpit.'

Henrietta clasped her hands in front of her. 'Oh! Charles. What is that? That building. Above all the others. It is exquisite.'

'Do you like it? Yes, I love it, too. It's the new Banqueting House. Inigo designed it. It was finished about three years ago. The old one burned down in a fire.'

'Ah, yes! Your most famous Inigo Jones!'

'Yes, indeed. But I worked with him on it. I work with him all the time. It's 55 feet wide and 55 feet high, a perfect Vetruvian double cube.'

'After Vetruvius?'

'Yes. Inigo thinks highly of Vetruvius. He is inspired by him.'

'Charles, it's amazing. Where did all those different coloured stones come from? We don't have that in France.'

'It was all brought in. The dark band at the bottom is from Oxfordshire, the honey-coloured stone is from Northamptonshire and the white is Portland stone.'

'You will be the envy of Europe if you can build like this. It must have cost a fortune.'

'It did. I think about £15,000 somebody said. But I don't care about all that. It is still not finished. Buckingham wants to bring Rubens in to put paintings on the interior ceiling.'

'Bravo!' She kissed him lightly on the cheek.

'Thank you, dear heart! But wait until you see the inside, even now. There is a huge room with no columns at all so the view is us uninterrupted when we put on masques.'

'Oh Charles! That's wonderful. And when will Inigo work on the new palace after you pull all this horrible mess down? Soon, I hope.'

Charles laughed. 'Yes, I very much hope so. He is one of the geniuses of our age, Inigo. He is an amazing man.'

'Can I work on the new palace, too? We could do it together.'

He stared at her. They were still surrounded by adoring crowds. It was still raining. 'Er , well, why not? Eh? Why not?'

'Why not indeed.'

Holding hands, they crossed King Street and went up the Privy Stairs into the Privy Garden. For the second time in her introduction to a new world, Henrietta was delighted by English horticulture. She and Charles walked slowly along gravel pathways lined with box hedges. The wallflowers were out, and poppies, tulips, roses and daises. She clapped her hands in delight.

'It's lovely. Oh, but where are the sculptures? You must commission my Hubert, Hubert le Sueur, to make graceful garden sculptures like we have at home. I mean...'

She looked at him, worried at the faux pas. He took her in his arms and kissed her, gently.

'You will love your new home, too. You will come to love it more. That is my solemn oath to you.'

A small garden led to Charles's apartments, in the south of the palace, soon to be known as The King's Side. Here, Charles showed Henrietta the Presence Chamber, with the throne and cloth of state. Henrietta baptised it with an approving nod. It was less dilapidated than everything else.

They crossed a lobby to the Privy Chamber where those of the rank of courtier met their king. To the left of this was the Withdrawing Chamber, the king's most private place.

To Charles's delight Henrietta asked about the paintings hanging here, which included Prince Henry's life-sized representation by the court painter, Daniel Mytens. This

149

had been painted after Henry's death from a miniature by Isaac Oliver, a miniaturist much loved by Charles. There were also life-sized pendant portraits, lovingly facing each other, of the exiled Elizabeth and her now languishing husband, Frederick. These were by Gerrit von Honthorst, who was with the couple now in The Hague.

Then they moved on, holding hands. Henrietta's apartments, soon to be known as The Queen's Side, were light and airy, overlooking a garden and the river. As he led her in to her own Withdrawing Room, Charles bade her shut her eyes, as he had a surprise for her.

She simpered with pleasure. He led her by the hand, stole a kiss on her lips, then said, 'Open your eyes now. I chose the paintings myself.'

Henrietta opened her eyes. The smile faded. She looked uncertain. Together, they looked at a painting of a plain, middle-aged man with full white beard and a long nose. He was wearing black armour and gauntlets and carrying a helmet. Behind him was the swagger of a red curtain.

'It's your father,' Charles said, softly. He was still holding her hand. 'It is Frans Porbus's portrait of him. There is another one of your father on horseback, by Léonard Gaultier. That is at Greenwich at the moment but I am having it hung in the First Privy Gallery here, so we can view it privately whenever we wish.'

Henrietta pulled her hand from Charles's. Then she flung her tiny frame at him with surprising force, wrapping her arms round him. Charles staggered, unbalanced. Henrietta moved her arms up to his neck and smothered his face with kisses.

'Oh, you wonderful man. Oh, I am so lucky.'

'No, no. Dear heart, I am fortune's favourite here. But tell me, my love, do you... Do you miss your father?'

She shrugged. 'I was only a baby when that mad pig François Ravaillac assassinated him. He stabbed him three times in his carriage. People told me about it, again and again, so even now I wake up screaming because I can see it in my dreams.'

'Oh my darling. I will heal your bad dreams with joy.'

She kissed him hard on the mouth. Then stared into his eyes.

'My first memory, you know? They took me, little baby me, to Papa's funeral. I was in the procession to St Denis. They held me over his body in the cathedral to sprinkle water on it from a *goupillon*. Mamanglat, I mean Madame de Montglat, Mamie's mother, put it in my hands. It felt cold. All the rooms at the Louvre were draped in black.'

'So sad. It is so sad, is it not?'

'All he wanted to do was do good for his people, my father. He built that salon where we met. He made lovely things in Paris.'

'His spirit was bringing us together.'

'Yes, we met while dancing. Well, *I* was dancing. I was dancing the Ballet Comique de la Reine, so beautifully. You were staring at my sister-in-law with your tongue out like that pig Buckingham.'

'Who? Anne? Me? No, no, no.' Charles was blushing, even though Henrietta's teasing was not true. He had hardly noticed Anne of Austria until Buckingham laid siege to her.

'In France, we used to have dancing and plays and masques all the livelong day long. My father was the patron of Ronsard, you know? He gave him a forest at Vendome for writing a sonnet. Isn't that romantic? And Corneille. The great Corneille. He wrote plays for our court gatherings.'

'I too wish to be a great patron of all the arts. It is my deepest, most heartfelt desire.'

'Good! We shall do it together.' She clapped her hands in glee. 'Masques. We must have masques like we had before at the Hotel de Rambouillet.'

'Oh, we have masques here, too.'

'You do? Oh yes, of course you do. You have Inigo Jones. Tomaso Francini, who designs our contrivances, says Mr Jones's stage machinery is very good. But I do not know your masques. What are your masques?'

'We had one just recently to celebrate our betrothal. Did you not know that?'

'No. Nobody told me. Nobody tells me anything. I am just a funny little Catholic girl with funny teeth.'

She stuck her teeth out like fangs. Charles laughed.

'The masque was called *The Fortunate Isles and Their Union*. I danced in it at the Banqueting House with our leading courtiers. Inigo exceeded himself with a wonderful device whereby an island moved to the front of the stage to join up with the shore, then receded to reveal a palace.'

'How marvellous!'

They discussed masques together, masques they knew or had danced in, then planning plans for new masques, but always absorbed in each other. Henrietta told Charles of a parlour game they used to play at St Germain-en-Laye. They used to retell fairy tales but putting each other in the stories. Henrietta as Cinderella with Gaston as the Prince was a favourite.

On and on Charles and Henrietta talked, giving each other their past selves totally. Both of them felt they might never leave that room again, as the rest of the world fell away.

But Endymion had made common cause with Madame de St Georges; they appeared together to let the royal couple know they were expected at the welcome banquet. Before they left, Henrietta whispered theatrically into Charles's ear.

'In my entourage, there is Bishop Mendy. I don't know if he is even really a bishop, he is too young. But do not trust him. He is Cardinal Richelieu's nephew. He reports to the Cardinal only. He is here to spy on you.'

The outside world had entered their kingdom.

## CHAPTER 20
### *THE PASTORAL LIFE*

Charles Stuart's coronation had been postponed for six months, to Candlemas Day in February of 1626, because of the plague, taking hold terribly in London. So Charles was not yet king, Henrietta not yet queen as she settled into her new life in an alien world.

After their first burst of bliss when she arrived in England, Charles continued to please her. He became a different person when she was there. He was lighter, he was fun, he told bad jokes. His nerviness and fears were banished to a dark realm.

He kept hold of her hand in a tight grip whenever they were together. He was holding onto her, in every sense, and she loved that. He gloried in public displays of affection, kissing her again and again in public, sometimes passionately. She suspected Charles enjoyed the disapproval this aroused in some of the more straight-laced courtiers, like Richard Weston, the Chancellor, who she disliked anyway.

She could afford some dislikes, as she had made many friends and allies among the courtiers. There was her friend Wat Montagu. There was Henry Jermyn. There was even the court beauty, Lucy Hay, Countess of Carlisle. They all took to her gaiety, not to mention her lovely singing voice which graced musical evenings. And they approved of her effect on Charles.

Buckingham entertained the royal couple at York House. He served sturgeon, which Henrietta was rather partial to. And she loved Katherine, his sparkling Catholic wife, making an ally and friend of her. Other banquets followed, in London high society; she was well received everywhere.

Without prompting from her, Charles began to discuss affairs of state with her – the war with Spain; Parliament's assaults on the power of the monarchy, usually expressed as attacks on Buckingham, as they dare not attack the monarchy directly.

He even mused about taking her with him for meetings of the Council of State, but she herself said that would be a step too far, not least as she would be unable to understand a word they were saying. When she pointed this out to him, they both fell about laughing.

One of her dislikes in London Charles found charmingly quirky: She hated eating in public, despite this requirement of 'good lordship' being part of the Bourbon Court she had come from. Her brother, Louis, often ate in public in the Louvre, but at sheltered St Germain-en-Laye it was unknown.

Henrietta expressed her feelings about the custom in art. Ten years later, she commissioned Gerard Houckgeest to paint her and Charles dining in public in Whitehall. Houckgeest knew what she wanted. He produced a cavernous room with a massive high ceiling. Tucked away on the left were two tiny figures at table, less than the size of toy soldiers but recognisable as Charles and Henrietta.

Standing behind them, watching as every mouthful went in, was a clutch of courtiers. Tiny figures of servants scurried to serve them, the clever tiled pattern of the painted floor emphasising how far they had to go. The painting did not show it but the food was invariably cold by the time it reached them.

The painting rendered the loneliness of majesty, the apartness of power. They had each other and only each other.

Food had been the site of another battle waged incessantly over Henrietta's first months in London. As early as that glorious first night of love at Dover Castle, Bishop Mendy and the Catholic retinue had tried to stop her eating the pheasant and venison at that afternoon's repast because it was a saint's day. Henrietta prevailed over Mendy then, eating her fill with gusto, and she prevailed later.

But they did not relent, those guardians sent to save not only her soul but the English souls around her. They persisted in badgering her to give up not only food but conjugal relations on every Saint's Day. Charles and Henrietta were lovers every night, the passion and pleasure of it was a revelation to her. Henrietta was firm. She refused Mendy's impertinent demand. Mendy's reports back to his uncle the Cardinal became one long expression of regret at her behaviour.


Henrietta had a propensity for sparkling mischief all her life, but since their childhood together Mamie St Georges was the spark that set her off. Mamie was blazingly loyal to Henrietta. She would have sacrificed her own life for her mistress in a heartbeat and both of them knew it.

Mamie was black-haired with an olive complexion. She was as tiny as Henrietta, pertly gamine and cheekily pretty. In her heart she recognised no hierarchies; Henrietta loved her for that.

It was Mamie's idea to disguise themselves and set off alone among the people – 'Your people' as Mamie put it to Henrietta. And what would they do among the people? Not talk to them, Mamie's English was rudimentary and Henrietta's still non-existent.

'We shall make purchases from various shops,' Henrietta announced.

But first they had to plan the outfit. Henrietta was all for the new style basqued bodice which looked like a male doublet. Hers was in lilac, tied at the waist by a ribbon sash. She found an identical outfit in blue satin for Mamie, both worn with a ruff. At the last minute, Henrietta found them both a pair of jersey silk tailored stockings, similar to those worn by men.

All dressed up, they admired themselves in the mirror. Then they admired each other. Then they admired each other in the mirror again. Then they fell to laughing for no discernible reason, other than happiness.

Where to go?

They had visited the New Exchange in the Strand, before. They knew Inigo Jones had designed the gracious building; England's new queen felt proud of that; it was now, in a manner of speaking, hers. Its two storeys of shops sold all sorts of beautiful objects from silver bound books to jewelled fans. But Henrietta, as always, craved the novel and the new.

'If there is a New Exchange, somewhere there must be an Old Exchange, n'est pas?' suggested Mamie. 'That's logical.'

Henrietta rang for one of her Ladies in Waiting. The call was answered by Lady Mary Villiers, Buckingham's mother. Henrietta got on surprisingly well with her, considering that Buckingham had put her there to report back to him on Henrietta's every movement.

Lady Mary thought the idea of them making purchases out in the street for themselves hilarious. She confirmed Mamie's deduction that if there was a New Exchange there must also be an Old Exchange.

'It dates from Elizabeth's time,' Lady Mary informed them. 'One of her courtiers, Thomas Gresham, built it. The clever man put a roof on it so the merchants would not get wet, as happened at their open-air meeting-place in Lombard Street.'

Henrietta was all for walking through London's streets to the Old Exchange, but Lady Mary ingeniously dissuaded her by pointing out possible damage to their shoes. She arranged a carriage for them.

The Old Exchange turned out to be near St Paul's. Instructing the driver and postilion to wait, Henrietta and Mamie made their way to the block of covered shops. There, the elegant and the gracious strode along the covered walkways, striking attitudes in colourful clothes, wishing to see and be seen.

With a cry of delight, Henrietta bought a little silver jewel box at the first shop they came to. Mamie explained to the shopkeeper that they were French ladies, visiting London. The shopkeeper, quite the gallant, kept bowing as if he were on a spring. He wished them a pleasant time in the capital.

Outside the shop, they shrieked with excitement at the transaction itself, at the box, and at the sheer novelty of being allowed to do something for themselves, rather than have one of a myriad servants do it.

'I want to buy something for Charles,' Henrietta said.

'Of course. What?'

'A miniature painting. He loves miniatures.'

They found a shop which dealt in paintings. The first miniature the shopkeeper showed her was perfect. It was an Isaac Oliver of Princess Elizabeth, Charles's beloved sister.

'Watercolour on vellum, Madam,' announced the shopkeeper solemnly. 'And if I may be so bold, I think her highness looks a treat. Perhaps we will have her back among us one day.'

Henrietta nodded, gathering the sense of what he said. Elizabeth's small-featured pretty face did indeed look a treat. Her swept-back hair showed the intelligence of her brow. It must have been painted just before her marriage to Frederick. She would have been about fourteen. But they did not have enough money to pay for it. Henrietta ordered it sent to her in Whitehall. The shopkeeper, with no flicker of surprise, bowed deeply.

'I will have it sent immediately, madam.'

There followed purchases for Mamie, ribbons and gloves and glazed fruits to which she was rather partial. Henrietta bought a pocket-watch for herself. She found a beaver hat which she thought would look good in a masque she was planning, a masque called *Artenice*. To her delight, she also found a stall selling Banbury Cakes. She had taken to this sweet English delicacy of honey, spices and rum.

The day passed half in and half out of their usual identities, with all the world open for them and willing for them to pick and choose what they wanted.

Henrietta and Mamie also made pastoral expeditions, exploring natural life in the country. At St Germain-en-Laye they had both loved the Maying expeditions. It was the same here in London.

She and Mamie, dressed simply à l'Anglaise, went on a Maying expedition by coach. When a bush was spied with its dense load of white pearly blossoms, they would give a cry, stop the coach, jump out, pick the early hawthorn branches and put them in their hats.

It reminded Henrietta of the Très Riches Heures of her girlhood. *Les Très Riches Heures du Duc de Berry* was a devotional book showing a calendar of the year with an illustration of the tasks performed in nature during that month.

May is represented by a joyous country ride with the women dressed in green, the colour of spring. The man in blue at the centre of the May picture is the Duc du Berry himself, the man who commissioned the devotional. But now Henrietta imagined it was Charles. Charles conducting the seasons, living attuned with nature. O how she loved him.

Summer saw Henrietta taking a rake and making hay with the haymakers along the Thames, breathing in the smells of lavender and hay. Although quite capable of Bourbon hauteur, especially toward nobles she considered lacking natural nobility, she loved rural simplicity and the people who lived their lives by it. She loved making hay, she loved having straw in her hair in the sunshine. She loved sharing the poor food of bread and pottage.

However, she was neither overly sentimental nor a fool; she knew how hard these people's lives were. But they were natural lives, that was the point. It is natural to live according to the rhythms of nature, ruled by sun and rain, river and mountain. To live in a packed and crowded heap in a city is not natural. She and Charles were at one on this. The pastoral masques they both loved were a celebration of this belief in the natural life.

# CHAPTER 21
## QUEEN HENRIETTA'S MEN

In the autumn of that same year, Charles gave Henrietta what she described through floods of tears to Mamie as 'the best birthday present a husband ever gave a wife'. Henrietta's birthday, like Charles's, was in November but by October the plague had eased sufficiently for the theatres to reopen. At which point Charles gave her his early present. He gave her her own theatre company, to be called Queen Henrietta's Men.

James had placed all the principal theatre companies under royal protection; under Elizabeth each had been under a different nobleman. Charles continued James's policy, forming his own company first called Prince Charles's Men, then the King's Men.

Charles arranged for one of the leading actors from the King's Men, Richard Perkins, to become the leading man in Henrietta's new company. The company was to be run by the experienced impresario Christopher Beeston, based at the Phoenix Theatre in Drury Lane.

Beeston had run a theatre company there for nearly a decade, one of fifteen vibrant companies in London. His resident dramatist, James Shirley, was transferred to the newly formed Queen Henrietta's Men.

Trembling with excitement, Henrietta shyly asked Charles if she could meet James Shirley. Could she visit the Phoenix? She had never seen, let alone visited, a public theatre before.

Charles, beaming at the success of his birthday gift said, 'Of course you can, dear heart. It's your company. Mr Shirley belongs to you.'

The very next evening they set off to attend a performance of Shirley's *The Maid's Revenge* at the Phoenix. They were promptly ensnared in a line of carriages snaking their way along King Street to Charing Cross. They slowed, then stopped.

Charles used the time to explain to Henrietta that Shirley and his ilk were professional playwrights, writing plays on demand to please an audience made up mainly of nobles. The nobles came to London from their country estates, put in a brief appearance at Parliament, usually to frame a Remonstrance complaining about the king, then attended the theatre in the evening.

The court masques were very different. They were closer to what Henrietta knew from France. They were more to do with art and music than words. What words there were tended to be written by court poets who would not expect to be paid for their efforts. They were written to please the king. They were watched by royalty, courtiers and foreign diplomats but then the scripts were printed and distributed for sale to the people up and down the land.

'Whaat! You sell the scripts of the masques? And the plays? And the people buy them, these scripts?'

'Some do, yes. Do you know of Robert Peake? He was Sergeant Painter to my father. He produced many paintings of my poor dear brother. When he died, his print-shop and copying studio were taken over by his son, William. William has made a great success of printing the scripts.'

'What is a copying studio?'

'William Peake has two copyists who copy works and restore paintings and repair frames and so on from a shop in the Strand. William Faithorne undertakes mainly engravings and one called William Dobson paints.'

'So many Williams. Will they copy paintings for me? I want to send a portrait of us to Gaston and Catherine at the same time. Mytens can do it.'

'Of course they will. Endymion will arrange everything for you.'

Henrietta listened to this wide-eyed. She was impressed by this spread of culture, outwards from the court, but was determined not to show it. By the time they arrived at the theatre the play had nearly finished but Beeston and James Shirley were waiting to meet them in Beeston's private quarters. These were behind the theatre, where a small repast of wine and tartlets had been laid on.

Beeston and Shirley bowed deeply to Henrietta and kissed her hand, which delighted her. Beeston was fair-haired, tall and rangy. He moved gracefully, like a fencer. He was steeped in theatre, born into it and knowing nothing but acting since his boyhood.

James Shirley was very different. Charles had told her he was a passionate royalist and a Catholic. He was a heavy man, redolent of weighty tomes, looking every pound the scholar he had been at both Oxford and Cambridge. His armchair appeared to have been carved round him, so snugly did it fit his form.

He had a round, heavy head dominated by a mole on his left cheek which moved when he spoke. It appeared to have an independent existence. Henrietta was fascinated by this blemish, resisting the temptation to catch it in her hand, as if it were alive. And then perhaps claim a prize for doing so.

Beeston to some extent but Shirley totally indicated that whatever Henrietta wished to see on the stage, they would write and perform.

'The theatre is a wit's market,' is how Shirley put it.

'How delightful!'

'Thank you, Your Majesty. I have a play brewing now which might interest you.' Shirley smiled as he spoke, the mole jumping about. His French was pretty good. 'It is entitled *The Cardinal*.'

Charles and Henrietta exchanged glances; Shirley was speaking through a faint smile. 'This Cardinal is always advancing his own interests. He fosters a marriage between two of the characters, I have called them Columbo and the

Duchess. But they resist his manipulations so he avenges himself on the Duchess by arranging her murder.'

The evening was turning into one of rich new experiences for Henrietta. The Cardinal? That could mean only Richelieu. In France they would not dare. Henrietta arched her eyebrows, mutely asking Charles what he thought.

'Go ahead,' Charles said, with unusual decisiveness. 'Leave Henry Herbert to me if there is a problem.'

Beeston smothered a smile. He already had Sir Henry Herbert, the Master of the Revels, in his pocket by means of regular bribes. Just that day he had bought Lady Herbert a lovely pair of calfskin gloves.

Nevertheless, Beeston and Charles were wary of Sir Henry because of the range of his powers. All plays had to be approved by him before performance. He could also issue safe passes protecting the actors from being pressed into the navy or the army, as long as they were registered to a theatre company. Sir Henry had already protected twenty-one of Henrietta's new troupe in this way. It would not be wise to alienate Sir Henry.

*The Cardinal* by James Shirley was produced at the Phoenix by Queen Henrietta's Men just one week later. It explicitly mentioned Richelieu in the prologue and was judged a big success. There was only one performance, as was usual. Bishop Mendy did not attend it but he reported it to Richelieu, who was incandescent. This was not what Henrietta Maria de Bourbon was supposed to be doing in England.

In revenge, Bishop Mendy, with ill-concealed delight, told Henrietta she could not take part in the coronation ceremony as it would be conducted by a Protestant bishop.

'But that means I will not be crowned Queen of England?'

Mendy shrugged and smirked. He was a lofty, well-made youth with a clear complexion. At times of emotion he tended to blush. He was blushing now.

'You may watch the ceremony from concealment when your husband is crowned.'

Where had this come from? Surely from a higher authority than Mendy? From Richelieu? From the Pope? From Louis? No, not Louis. Her brother would not be so vindictive. He lacked the energy for any high emotion.

She blinked back tears, determined not to show he had hurt her. 'So am I Queen of England, or am I not?'

Mendy shrugged again, relishing the discomfiture of this broken reed who had so refused to do the bidding of her religion. 'You must ask a secular authority,' he said, loftily. 'I am an ecclesiastical authority.'

She thought: you are the nephew of your uncle and that is all. But she said nothing.

Charles's coronation was held on a bitter February day with bulging snow clouds hanging lower than the ceilings of palaces, or so it appeared. Henrietta did indeed watch from concealment, as Mendy had permitted. She and Mamie St Georges sat swathed in black in a closed carriage with a small window. Charles had made the arrangements. He was as distraught as Henrietta that she was not to be by his side on Coronation Day.

Before the coronation proper, Charles had insisted on taking the sacrament as a sign of the purification of the new reign after the licentiousness of James's time as king. This was a private, indeed a secret ceremony, as the Puritans would see it as a sign of 'Popery' and no doubt blame Henrietta for it.

The rite was to be at the Church of St Clement Dane, hard by Covent Garden. The small congregation sang thirteen parts of the 119th psalm, but as they did so a terrible event occurred.

The Reverend Jacob, the Minister, collapsed with a fever and began to babble and rave even as he gave the sacrament. The congregation gasped, muttered, some shrieked as it became clear the wretched divine had the plague. He was taken home and died after languishing in agony for five days.

That was the most dreadful of omens for the reign. When James was crowned in 1603, there had also been a terrible plague. And now this, just before Charles's coronation. Was the Stuart dynasty cursed?

The small knot of witnesses to the event were sworn to secrecy. Buckingham was there. And Endymion Porter. And Wat Montagu. Henry Jermyn and Thomas Howard,

Lord Arundel. All of them could be relied upon not to spread the story further.

Sir Richard Weston had also been present, the Chancellor of the Exchequer. He was hastily instructed to make a large payment to the Reverend Jacob's family to ensure their silence. Charles was a naturally secretive man who did not trust his fellow human beings easily. He was pleased this particular secret was so well sealed it remained closed to public knowledge.

Charles and his coterie of courtiers took their carriages from St Clement Dane back to Whitehall, shadowed by Henrietta's sealed coach. From there, they headed the procession to Westminster Abbey. Charles walked under a canopy supported on silver staves carried by his small circle of intimates. The choir sang a prayer wishing him long life. It was the same prayer sang at James's coronation.

Charles had chosen to wear a suit of white satin, modelled on Buckingham's, although he had a purple mantle over it. He was the first king not to wear all-purple at his coronation. Charles was trying to show his soul was pure, white, untouched. But for many the colour recalled a prophecy by William Lilly, a savant learned in astrology. Lilly's Prophecy of the White King and the Dreadful Dead Man tells of a prince in white who becomes 'lost to the eye of the world and to the love and affections of his people'.

John Donne, Dean of St Pauls, took the theme of martyrdom for his first sermon to the new king: 'The last thing Christ bequeathed to thee was his blood, refuse not to go to him the same way too, if his glory requires the sacrifice'.

Charles then swore the same oath his father had sworn, surrounded by the medieval relics of Edward the Confessor. This was an attempt to establish the nascent, struggling Stuart dynasty as worthy successors.

The glories of the wondrous reign of the Protestant heroine Elizabeth were everywhere seen in roseate hue. But then had come a limping debauched figure from Scotland who cared for nothing but reading and hunting. And now his son, equally unprepossessing physically, towing the twin burdens of a hated Chief Minister and a Catholic queen with a bloated Catholic retinue who was there to promote Catholicism and who spoke no English.

At the coronation, Charles was given the crown, the symbol of the people's love. He was handed the sceptre representing royal authority. And he was anointed in cruciform, imprinting him with God's mark. The anointment was with oil scented with orange and jasmine – Charles's choices.

A coronation, it was commonly believed, made a new person, not only a new king. The new person had been chosen by God, so was touched with the divine.

As Charles stepped outside the abbey after the coronation ceremony that bitterly cold February day, it began to snow. It was light at first, a flurry of powder snow. A cold wind whipped it into a funnel and the funnel of snow settled round the king. The white snow settled into his white face and covered his white suit, masking his outline. Henrietta, watching from the window of her carriage, screamed.

On the day of his coronation, the fear from the depths of his soul, the fear that was his first memory in Dunfermline Palace, came to pass. As the snow settled all over him, Charles Stuart disappeared.

# CHAPTER 23
## A MOLLUSC IN ITS SHELL

Charles was ready to make changes to the court. One day, his royal court would be housed in one of the great palaces of civilisation. It would be a wonder to behold. Meanwhile, he would work with what he had, Whitehall Palace.

First, the people. The people, those few close to him, always came first. The loyal Endymion Porter's stipend as Groom of the Bedchamber was increased to a wildly generous £500 a year for life. All the musicians from Charles's court as Prince of Wales and from the new court as king, including a separate group called The Musicians for Lutes and Voices, were placed under the Master of Music, Nicholas Lanier.

Henrietta asked Charles to retain her French lutenist and lute teacher, Jacques Gaultier. Charles did not really want to do this. Gaultier had joined the court as a protégé of Buckingham. Charles knew he had been at Louis's court and there were rumours he had fled a charge of murder there.

It was not unusual for those charged with some delict at the French court to find sanctuary in England and vice versa. But Charles felt intimidated by Gaultier's air of sophisticated confidence. He was also jealous of his ability to make Henrietta laugh. They always appeared to have some secret, some shared knowledge in chatty idiomatic French, which excluded him.

Gaultier was a round-faced elegantly moustachioed fellow with a burning bush of unruly hair, crackling out from all sides of his head. He was not good-looking exactly, but there was a power there, an inner force which spoke of passion.

But Charles certainly had to admit to himself that Gaultier was one of the foremost lutenists in the world.

He had designed the double-necked lute he played so beautifully. He had made another one for Henrietta, which flattered her immensely. They played duets of his composition on them – alone and in private.

Nevertheless, Charles was persuaded to confirm Gaultier's appointment as a lutenist under Nicholas Lanier and as Henrietta's private lute teacher.

The other priority was art. Charles promised an annual subsidy of £2,000 to the tapestry factory at Mortlake, so that it could compete with and hopefully surpass the great Flemish workshops. He retained the Dutch court artist, Daniel Mytens, on a salary of £420 each for all paintings, even though he was lukewarm about the standard of art Mytens produced.

Then there was the court itself. To Charles, the court should be a world in miniature of how England should live. He was convinced the court's example would find its way to the people, given time.

Not only would the licentiousness of James's court be ended, so would the near permanent state of war with either Spain or France so the privateers could boost the exchequer by robbing their ships. As his first public act, Charles banned swords, boots and spurs from the palace. He wished to be a king who promoted peace, not merely talk about it, as James had.

Within his peace the arts would flourish. So would the rural ways advocated by Spenser in *The Shepherd's Calendar*. The old pastimes were to be reintroduced; dancing, the May Games, archery, wakes wassails, all the Merrie England pastimes the Puritans wanted banned as disorders.

However, Charles frowned on bull or bear baiting. They were violent and cruel; both were banned. Charles had not forgotten the bear torn to pieces by lions in the Tower which his father made him witness when he first came to London.

Many of the rural pastimes Charles favoured were set out in a book published in James's time, *The Book of Sports*. Charles had it reprinted as a model of how courtiers should behave. But the primary model for emulation was the masque, with its attendant anti-masque showing the chaos that ensued if the peaceful rural ways were not followed.

To Charles, it was axiomatic that a court embodying these ideals could evolve only if access to it were limited to people who lived by these ideals. He therefore promulgated voluminous lists of exactly who was allowed exactly where in the court. The double locks on the doors were replaced by triple locks. There were detailed regulations as to who could enter which room when and what they could do once inside.

He limited contact as far as possible to the small coterie of people who did not intimidate him, with some inevitable exceptions like Jacques Gaultier. The lists themselves, however, taken out of the context of their purpose, led to the charge of authoritarianism frequently levelled at Charles. It was a charge he found perplexing.

When Henrietta first arrived, Charles had shown her the circles of his armoured private world. First, the Presence Chamber, then the Privy Chamber, then the Withdrawing Room. Charles was like a soft and helpless mollusc building himself concentric layers of outer shell.

Henrietta was soon obsessed and consumed by a project, a delightful plan, a gift for Charles. She would stage a pastoral, a masque in the French style known as *précieuses* which she had first seen as a girl of six at the salon of the Marquise de Rambouillet.

Here, a great lady would give her benison to a coterie of servants who in return would immortalize her in verse. So early in her plans Henrietta determined to invite all the artisans who would create the masque to watch the finished performance. This had never been done in England or in France, which made it all the more attractive to her.

She chose the pastoral *Arténice* by Honorat de Bueil, sieur de Racan, who had been a page at her father's court. She had seen it performed at the French court again six years ago and wished to replicate that performance as closely as possible. She herself would take the leading role and a dozen of her French ladies would take the other speaking roles.

The English ladies, especially Lucy Hay, Duchess of Carlisle, and the Marchioness of Hamilton, were only too glad to join in the dancing in the pastoral sections of the masque. Lucy Hay and Henrietta were becoming close. The louche court beauty showed the gawky girl how to use make-up, how to dress with style, how to flirt.

But the first step in the realisation of a masque was always to enlist the famous Inigo Jones to design the stage sets. Henrietta met him in her rooms on the Queen's side of Whitehall. At first she feared that Inigo would be unable or unwilling to adapt to French styles. After five minutes with him, his small eyes unwavering on her face as if he were reading a book, she realised how misplaced this fear was.

She understood, as Charles had, that Inigo's undoubted genius was not as an innovator but as an adapter, often of Vitruvius or other classic masters. His adaptations incorporated adjustments and alterations to the template being imitated at the planning stage, everything edged towards the needs of the present commission. There was then a superlative execution and realisation of the plan in action.

Inigo's stiff jutting beard bobbed as he nodded understanding of what was required, occasionally making notes, usually in the form of ad hoc sketches. Henrietta started to enjoy his intense immersion in her project. Together, they planned seven changes of scenery and what they hoped would be breath-taking sound and light effects.

The pastoral would open with a moonlit village scene, which Inigo based on an engraving by Serlio. This was to be transformed into a wood, then, after a dramatic storm, the moon would appear over a mountain. The pastoral element would then be succeeded by the masque proper, involving a painted backdrop showing the Thames and what was soon to be Henrietta's new home, Somerset House.

Charles was kept away from the extensive preparations for Henrietta's masque. He was delighted by them, though nagged by perturbing doubt. In his mother's day a queen could dance on the stage, as indeed Anne of Denmark often had. But times were changing. The Puritans had begun their dark and sinister march. Dancing on stage would be a ready excuse to attack the Catholic queen.

Also, Henrietta and some of her ladies were dancing male roles dressed in doublet and hose, some even with false beards. This had not been seen even in James's reign. It was daring. It risked provoking the Puritans to even greater depths of righteousness.

So there were no drumrolls in advance of *Arténice*. On the day of the performance, only a few foreign diplomats were invited and no arrangements were made to print the masque, which would have needed translation anyway.

Charles found out about the artisans being in the audience only when he arrived in the evening. There they sat, looking slightly bemused, to one side of the stage.

George Gellin Taylor had made nineteen gowns for the queen and her attendants. George Binion, sitting next to him, had provided 1,475 ounces of gold and silver bone and lace to trim Mr Taylor's gowns. John Sturton had provided thirteen beaver hats, Hugh Pope seven pairs of garters, John Morrell had provided cambric for the ruffs. Even Ralph Grynder, known as an upholsterer, which meant interior designer, had been employed to make soft seats on the edge of Inigo's set for the pastoral.

The artisans talked loudly among themselves about payment. None of them had yet been paid in full and some not at all. But when they saw Inigo's Italian village backdrop receding into the distance past the proscenium they fell silent and gasped. How had it been done? Each of them thought the scene real, a model, none of them admitted that to the others.

But for Charles and for the foreign diplomats it was Henrietta who was the refulgent star in the world she had created. She was by far the best dancer; graceful, lithe and acrobatic. And Charles appreciated the considerable achievement of her learning and delivering six hundred lines of French verse faultlessly.

The day after the performance, the artisans, acting together, resubmitted outstanding bills. Charles tut-tutted with impatience at this. He did not concern himself with money. He was the king, was he not? He was appointed by God's will, fantastical though that seemed to him. Very well then, England could find him the money for whatever he happened to need. Or more precisely the Chancellor of the Exchequer could.

Charles shared Henrietta's dislike of Sir Richard Weston, though he was rather more circumspect about showing it. Weston was nervy, which made Charles's own nerves worse. He was a clerk like figure with the narrowest horizons Charles had ever encountered.

Like Buckingham, Endymion Porter and Charles himself, Weston's wife was a Catholic. Puritans would therefore automatically charge him with being a puppet of Papists, furthering the Catholic interest, whatever he did. This made Weston even more nervous than he was already.

Henrietta said Weston reminded her of a burrowing mole. She wrinkled her nose at the sight of him. He compounded her dislike by clumsily over-transparent attempts to soft-soap her. He could not bring himself to attend the court masques, but he attempted flattery by asking Henrietta about them in shaky French.

Then he commissioned a Hubert Le Sueur bronze statue of Minerva for the grounds of his estate in Essex. This was accompanied by a blatantly insincere pretence of interest in sculpture generally, and specifically in the work of French sculptors, and especially Le Sueur, who just happened to have come to England as Henrietta's protégé.

And now the wretched Weston had asked to see him, Charles. No doubt about money. Charles received him, formally, in the Presence Chamber. Weston shrewdly began with the item Charles was most likely to agree with.

'Bouge of court, your Majesty.' Weston tended to mumble in half-sentences, as if stopping before somebody stopped him.

'What about it?'

Bouge of court was the right to eat at the king's expense at court. Once awarded it was seldom withdrawn. It usually extended to all meals and as much as the lucky recipient could drink.

'Hundreds of people,' Weston mumbled.

'Do we know how many, exactly?'

'I'm afraid not, Your Majesty. But if your Majesty wishes...'

'Yes, alright. Anything else?'

'If it pleases Your Majesty, having identified them, many could instead of bouge of court be put on board wages. Essentially, a fixed amount...'

'Good idea.'

'And I have instructed the Treasurer to purchase at the cheapest price and I am even now engaged on a study of the number of carts assigned to each department on a progress.'

'Splendid.'

'Yes.'

'Why do we never have any money for the masques?'

Weston cleared his throat. 'Parliament has seen fit to approve the war with Spain, but without granting any money for it, either last year or this year. And...'

'And?'

'The exchequer was some million pounds in debt on the death of your late, sainted father, God rest his soul.'

'A million? How did it get to... to...'

Weston hesitated. The daily ration allowance for the king alone was £25 5s 4d. Two thousand people could live on that for a year. The royal household cost £260,000 a year. If he chanced mentioning the king's own expenditure, especially on masques, His Majesty would simply find another Chancellor. Weston was nervous enough about his position anyway, without taking such a huge risk.

But there was something else. With the occasional rashness of the permanently fearful he plunged on: 'A significant proportion of wealth is going to the maintenance of your sister's court in the Hague, Your Majesty. There is an annual pension, as it is described, of £18,000 plus regular disbursements of £1,000 apparently for extra servants.'

'Fair enough. If Elizabeth and Frederick need it. You are not to touch that.'

'Yes, Your Majesty. I mean no Your Majesty. I feared you would say that. And then of course there are your own palaces and castles. You have nineteen in all.'

'Good Lord!'

Weston's recklessness was turning to anger – a weak man's anger, a tetchy petulance not unlike Charles's own. He flushed, dropping his eyes, unwilling to meet Charles's gaze. 'And they all require tapestries, paintings, plate and furniture.'

'Are you suggesting I live without furniture, Weston?'

Weston shook his head vigorously. 'Indeed not. No. But...'

'But?'

Weston saw he must change the subject. 'There are measures we can take. We have, with the aid of the Royal Jeweller, Mr Duarte, managed to pawn the Crown Jewels in Holland.'

'Whaat?'

'Yes. Otherwise we would have run out of money completely. The coronation would have been impossible. So would Her Majesty's entertainment, *Arténice*. I thought I had better apprise Your Majesty of that knowledge.'

'Yes. Thank you, Weston.'

Charles gleefully reported his vanquishing of the pettifogging clerk – that is Weston – to Henrietta. Henrietta praised him, hugged him, kissed him. She was physical with him, rough even, adding passion and desire to the rough-and-tumble with Gaston and the other boys of her girlhood.

Whenever they were together they were touching, hugging, holding hands and kissing. They believed they had reached a Platonic whole of unity, though certainly not the pallid Platonic love, passionless, so much in vogue.

There was another facet of their love, which he found curious, though delightful. Without asking permission from either Charles himself or his doctors, she took charge of his treatment for rickets.

After unceremoniously stripping him in the Privy Chamber, Henrietta would apply Charles's regular poultice of mallows and rye bran boiled up with wine and vinegar. The only other soul Charles had allowed this intimacy was Buckingham, who had applied this same poultice when Charles was suffering on the journey through France and Spain. Even Elizabeth had never laid hands on him in this manner, not even when they were children together in Scotland.

Charles and Henrietta seldom quarrelled, but their quarrels were incendiary when they did occur. She would launch herself at him, beating and berating him, tiny fists clenched, screaming like a banshee. He learned to yell back, admitting to himself afterwards he felt better for it.

The cause of the quarrels was nearly always the same: the bloated numbers of the French court. But Charles saw another side to the same problem. Henrietta still had learned hardly a word of English. Bodily, she was in England but her soul and spirit were stubbornly back in France. Not being crowned queen of England had made this worse. For her own happiness, Charles knew, the retinue had to go. She had to start to become English, with the influences from France diminished if not eliminated.

When this glowing ember of dissatisfaction finally burst into flame, the spark was Buckingham. He had already successfully planted influential English court ladies into Henrietta's court retinue, like Lady Carlisle, and his mother, Mary Villiers. It was a bonus that Henrietta actually liked them both.

Parliament saw the matter differently. They saw Buckingham and his mother in league with the Popish queen whose strings he was pulling like a puppet. They sought to question Buckingham, as ever undermining Charles through his courtiers.

Parliament then impeached Buckingham. He was charged with treason by way of his reckless squandering of the king's treasure on superfluous feasts, magnificent buildings, riots and excesses. He was also accused of poisoning James during His Majesty's final illness. He would end his days in the Tower if this impeachment succeeded.

Buckingham's many enemies rallied to Parliament's cause. His sworn enemy, John Digby, Earl of Bristol, had not forgotten the humiliating way Buckingham had treated him on arrival in Madrid. He emerged from retirement to accuse Buckingham of deliberately wrecking the Spanish marriage and a possible Spanish alliance because of his infatuation with the French queen, Anne of Austria.

He further accused Buckingham of not conducting proper negotiations with Spain's representative, Peter Paul Rubens, but instead vainly having his portrait painted and extravagantly negotiating the purchase of paintings for his home.

Charles was nonplussed. Only a speedy reduction of French influence at court could assuage Parliament. Buckingham's mother, Mary Villiers chose this of all moments to try and tighten her hold over Henrietta. She tried to get the Marchioness of Hamilton (Buckingham's niece) and the Countess of Denbigh (Buckingham's sister) added to the list of Ladies in Waiting.

Henrietta, seething, drew up a counter-list of women she wanted as Ladies in Waiting and presented it to Charles. Charles, typically, did not read the list. He did not read anything he did not like. In compensation, he read anything he did like obsessively, repeatedly and so comprehensively he nearly always annotated the text. He did this with copies of Shakespeare's plays and the inventory of royal artworks.

Without thinking, Charles said, 'I will be master in my own house,' as Henrietta's list slid off a table onto the floor.

Fists clenched, Henrietta said, 'All I am asking for is the same authority over my staff that your mother enjoyed.'

'There is no comparison between you and my mother.'

'No, you are right. I am a Bourbon princess not the ruler of some backwater in the north.'

Charles stormed out. The next time he saw her he said he was sending all her entourage back to France for her own good and that of the nation.

'What about Mamie?'

'Her too. It is for the best.'

'Charles, no! I cannot live without her. I have never been without her. That is savage and cruel. You unnatural husband!'

He winced. 'It... it... will help you over the years.'

In the end, the Yeomen of the Guard were called to clear out the French, using force if necessary. It was necessary. The queen's ladies howled and yelled, as did Mendy in particular and many of the priests.

Mendy had already told Henrietta, many times, that she was a poor servant of the True Faith and that his reports to Richelieu had made that clear. He had called her *timide et craintifre* – timid and fearful – and her closeness to Charles had been condemned.

Eventually, thirty or so carriages and carts were lined up in the courtyard. Mamie St Georges looked up through streams of tears to see her mistress and the English king fighting at a window, for all the world like Punch and Judy at a show. Henrietta was banging her fists against the glass. To Mamie's horror the glass then shattered, leaving Henrietta striking her husband with bleeding hands.

Charles half relented and half repented after the quarrel. The French had left Whitehall but they were still in the country. It was announced that Henrietta could keep a nurse, a cook, a baker and Hubert le Sueur, the sculptor.

She was also given a priest and a new Lady in Waiting to replace Mamie St Georges. Her name was Madame Vantelet. Charles had made sure she could speak English well and she had been instructed to use English with Henrietta as often as possible.

After the quarrel, Charles and Henrietta had their most passionate night of love. She assumed the dominant role in their lovemaking.

# CHAPTER 26
## THE GREATEST ART COLLECTION IN THE WORLD

Charles prided himself on being more than an art collector. He was an art connoisseur. He enjoyed being called a virtuoso – someone who appreciated and was knowledgeable about art. All who knew him thought he was worthy of the title. Rubens called him the greatest amateur of painting among the princes of the world – and Rubens knew just about every prince in the world.

When Henry died, Charles inherited over a hundred paintings, with more than a hundred and fifty coming to him on the death of his mother. These formed the basis of one of the foremost art collections in Europe. It was elevated yet further by the paintings acquired on the Spanish adventure. But Charles wanted more. He wanted much more.

His collection to date, with the much-loved purchases from Spain prominent, hung mainly in the scattered galleries of Whitehall: The Bear Gallery, the Adam and Eve Stairs Room, the Privy Lodgings Room, the Privy Gallery, Charles's own bedroom and the Long Gallery which ran at right angles off the bedroom. Additionally, some pieces, mostly less favoured, were at St James's Palace, Greenwich or Windsor Castle.

Acquisitions were added piecemeal, with those closest to his heart hung closest to Charles physically in his hermetically sealed world. They were all inventoried by Abraham van der Doort, Surveyor of the King's Pictures, a careworn Dutchman.

Van der Doort was still a handsome man, although at some twenty years older than Charles he looked like a magnificent-prowed galleon just smashed on rocks. Shoulder-length hair, a bushy beard just holding its shape, a proud prow of a nose. But there was sadness in the flinching eyes and the surrender to bitterness in the mouth.

The inventory of art works he kept was frequently annotated by Charles in his tiny writing. He would make additions and corrections, make new demands and ask questions, which drove the ageing van der Doort to distraction.

Charles was engaged in yet more annotations, with a fretting van der Doort at his shoulder, when Endymion brought him the most exciting news of his life. One of the largest and most glorious art collections in the world was to be put on the market intact. It was the collection of the Gonzaga family of Mantua.

Charles's eyes shone. 'What do we know of it, Endymion?'

Endymion smiled. 'It is unique in all the world, Your Majesty. Mantegna's *Triumph of Caesar* is among the works. Also pieces by Raphael, Titian and Correggio. The extent is yet to be determined. But certainly hundreds of paintings and scores of sculptures.'

Abraham van der Doort shifted uneasily on aching feet, ignored and ill at ease. Charles was soaring.

'The Gonzaga family! They were characters in Castiglione's *The Book of the Courtier.* Well, some of them were. Our old tutor, Henry Peacham, schooled us in it, Henry and me. It sets out the courtly ideal we should live by. It is written as a dialogue between characters.'

Endymion nodded his heavy head in ponderous agreement.

Charles was transported back to childhood. Lessons in the library with Henry Peacham. Charles and Henry used to let him come upon them unawares as they pretended to be reading *The Gentleman's Exercise*, one of his own books, which they would then extravagantly praise in his hearing.

'What a fine book this is, Charles.'

'Among the finest I have every read, Henry.'

'Who could have written such a fine... Oh hello, Mr Peacham, sir. We did not see you standing there.'

Henry Peacham beamed. The dreamy old man fell for the ruse every time. He was delighted they were reading his book.

Henry Peacham, a white-haired albino rabbit with rheumy eyes, broke off to burrow among the books, manuscripts and pictures he had laboriously brought in to the library with him. He found what he was looking for and laid it reverently on the big oak table between the boys.

'*The Book of the Courtier* was both inspired by and includes, as a character in the dialogues which form the book, Elisabetta Gonzaga of the distinguished and noble Gonzaga family of Mantua. And here she is, my noble gentlemen, Elisabetta Gonzaga in an etching by Raphael. In life she was praised for her fortitude and virtue.'

Peacham unrolled the etching and held it up to view. He fell silent while Charles and Henry examined the noble brow, large eyes and straight patrician nose of Elisabetta Gonzaga of Mantua.

After a few moments, the tutor broke the silence: 'In terms of the lessons we must learn for our own times, the courtly ideal is the Country Gentleman who stays on his manor, not visits once a year from the city like a cuckoo in the spring, leaving the upkeep of the land to the yeomen. I believe today's courtiers, for your example in England, are men such as Sir Philip Sidney, Francis Bacon, Richard Hooker and Samuel Daniel, who wrote *Tethys Festival*, the masque with which we shall welcome Prince Henry as Prince of Wales.'

'It will be my honour,' said Henry, solemnly.

Charles had tears in his eyes as the memory faded. 'Oh, Endymion it should have been Henry. It should have been Henry buying these treasures, not me.' Yet again he wondered how it could possibly be God's will that he was king.

James's funeral had been in May 1625. Early in June, Charles had sent Nicholas Lanier to Venice to purchase paintings. It was his first act as king. So Lanier was the natural choice to make haste from Venice to Mantua to buy the Gonzaga collection.

As well as being Master of the King's Music, Nicholas Lanier was a gifted painter who understood the art world. His self-portrait, in a black doublet and a plain white collar, has both a palette and a sheet of music. It shows him with a moustache and a bearded chin, not unlike Charles's. But he has a quizzical look, twinkling eyes and his hat is set at a rakish angle – a man amused by life and ready to play his part in it, not apprehensive and watchful, like Charles.

Lanier's French ancestry is discernible in his face. The Laniers were Gascon originally, from Rouen. Nicholas's father and grandfather had been established court musicians. He was thirty-seven at the time of the Gonzaga commission.

When the letter arrived at his quarters in Venice, informing him of his role as an art purchaser, Lanier's customary sang-froid vanished. His eyes opened wide. His reaction was one of blank terror. He wrote back to Endymion: 'Since I came into the world I have made famous contracts but never a more difficult one than this.'

To Charles, life was straightforward, details an irritation. His will should be done. But Nicholas Lanier understood immediately that a massive undertaking like the Gonzaga purchase would require an established dealer, versed in the skills of negotiating, money transfer, packing and shipping. Such men dwelt in the complex, shady and convoluted world of art dealing, with its tangled webs of connections often interlinked with spying.

He needed the main agent in Italy, one Daniel Nijs, who ran his complex networks of deals from an office in

Venice, with a warehouse in nearby Murano. Nijs was a Calvinist, a clear-eyed, sharp dealer for whom paintings were judged solely by their value.

Mantua lies on the flat plains of Lombardy, surrounded by lakes and the Mincio River. The collection was displayed in the Galleria della Mostra where Mantegna's *Triumphs of Caesar*, nine crowded and brave battlefield paintings, was prominent. Mantegna had been court painter in Mantua in 1460. Rubens regarded him as his great predecessor when he became court painter in Mantua himself, for four years.

Charles was playing no part in any selection within the Gonzaga collection. Lanier had complete discretion. He and Daniel Nijs negotiated, at first at least, with Duke Ferdinando Gonzaga, a former cardinal in Rome, a veteran of one of the most difficult, cosmopolitan art markets in Europe. The first complication occurred when he died, to be succeeded by his younger brother, Duke Vincenzo II. Negotiations had to start again from the beginning.

The money, in the form of Bills of Exchange, that Charles had initially sent Nicholas Lanier to live on, had run out. Nijs was paying for Lanier's board in Mantua, but he was beginning to run out of money himself.

Duke Vincenzo insisted on selling the collection as a whole, indeed he stipulated that it must be kept together even after sale. He eventually gave permission for it to be shipped back to England in more than one batch, but even that only after fierce negotiation.

The cost for the whole collection was a massive £15,000, which Vincenzo was insisting be paid at once, not over a period of time in instalments. Lanier, known by now all over Mantua as 'the blond Englishman', was getting letters from Charles saying there was no money available at the moment.

This was at least partly because Buckingham needed what finance there was for an expedition. He had a pet project to send a fleet to support the French Huguenots who were coming under attack from Louis at the Breton port of La Rochelle. Charles's heart was with the Gonzaga purchases, but good governance indicated support for Buckingham's war effort. As ever, he was reluctant to let Buckingham down.

Weston had told Charles he could have his art collection or the expedition but not both. Endymion partly solved the conundrum by going to Arundel, who was a patron of Lanier's, and obtaining a loan from him. While Endymion, with help from Lanier, worked at unpicking the London knots, negotiation with the Mantuans was left entirely to Nijs.

There were approximately two thousand paintings in the collection. The first Mantuan inventory left out some of the best. Nijs insisted on another inventory. This time, some of the leading gems of the collection, Raphael's *La Perla* and Correggio's two allegories, *The Allegory of Vice* and *The Allegory of Virtue* were included.

In the face of all this horse-trading and skulduggery, Nicholas Lanier retreated into music. Monteverdi had lived in Mantua until 1613. His operas were frequently performed there. Lanier attended a superb performance of *L'Arianna*. He was moved to tears by the wonderful lamento, which he wrote to Charles about. He even managed to find a copy of the manuscript and eventually brought it back to England with him.

Meanwhile, Duke Vincenzo was insisting that every painting in the collection must be copied before it was sold. Copies were nearly always made of paintings before they were sold, but given the size of the collection the buyer could be waiting for years.

Lanier and Nijs were saved by the political situation. Mantua was strategically significant, lying due south of the Brenner Pass, controlling access to the Italian peninsula to the north. Vincenzo weakened as he feared Mantua may come under attack and the collection be lost completely.

The attack actually materialised after the pictures were sold. They would have been looted. Duke Vincenzo abandoned the demand for copies.

When the sale was finally agreed, the remaining issue was transportation. Usually, paintings would be transported overland, as this was far safer. But the sheer size of the Mantua collection made this impossible.

Nijs arranged sea transport for the bulk of the purchases from the Venetian Lido to London aboard a 100-ton ship called the *Margaret*. The *Margaret* was manned by a crew of just thirty-seven mariners, to save money. What little money there was left went on customs waivers, as Byzantine an affair as even Nijs had ever negotiated.

Nijs knew very well that the crew of the *Margaret* was neither large enough nor experienced enough in transporting precious cargo, but he literally could not afford to spend any more time on work he was not being paid for.

Meanwhile, Lanier set off by land, in a train of carriages carrying some of the best pieces from the collection. These included works by Raphael, Tintoretto, Titian and the two Correggios, which were water colours and easily damaged by the sea. It was arranged that Lanier and his precious load would return to London via Antwerp, as Charles wished him to visit van Dyck in his studio. He had a message for the Dutchman, via Lanier – an offer of work.

# CHAPTER 27
## ANTHONY VAN DYCK

Nicholas Lanier had great anticipation of his meeting with Anthony van Dyck again after what? six years, perhaps a little more. The note he had received from the artist summed up all his jangling vulnerable warmth. It had arrived just before Lanier left Venice, having supervised the loading of large parts of the Gonzaga collection aboard the *Margaret*.

'It will do my heart good to see you again,' Anthony had written, in French. 'Send me your best court clothes ahead by the fastest means, so I can paint you in all your finery and so please our master.'

So van Dyck knew the portrait of Nicholas Lanier was to be his selling point for an offer of a court post from His Majesty. That was good news. But the request for his best clothes was a surprise.

Apart from his self-portrait, there was only one other portrait of himself. It was by the younger van Steenwyck, Hendrick, showing Lanier the musician. In this portrait, his long handsome face, full-bearded this time, was thin; his body downright skinny. He looked out at the viewer while playing the lute. You could even see which chord he was playing. On a side table was pen and paper. This symbolised more artistic endeavour. Lanier also wrote poetry, as most people did.

This approach in the Steenwyck portrait was what he would have expected, showing Lanier the – possibly hungry – musician. Van Dyck's request for his finest clothes, to be painted before Lanier's arrival, surely meant he was going to show Lanier as a courtier. Lanier smiled to himself as his carriage approached Antwerp. It was typical of Anthony's warm generosity.

He peered out of the window of his carriage – open curiosity at life, meeting it, by and large, with a smile. Over there was the cathedral tower. Inigo must have loved that when he was in Antwerp. Then more spires, one of which must be St Walburgiskerk. That chunky block must be a prison. And there are the fortifications, along the waterfront. The triangular gabled windows of the houses were like the sails of ships, strangely beautiful.

When they came to a halt, Lanier stiffly disembarked. He breathed in the salt air, leaning against the side of the carriage. Then came the chore of storing fifty or so paintings and some sculptures in one of the many massive waterside wharves along the Scheldt on Antwerp's waterfront.

The casual efficiency of the Flemish storemen both pleased and repulsed him as they stored the Mantua treasures among the Caribbean sugar, south American gold and silver, Baltic grain and timber, Flemish cloth, German wine, English tin and textiles and the Good Lord knew what else.

Lanier wanted to shout at them, 'These are the finest fruits of civilisation. This is the apogee of human endeavour.' But realised the gnarled, muscular Flemings were best left alone to pack and store the treasures as they saw fit, even if that included tossing them from hand to hand.

But finally Lanier was free to call on Anthony again. Suffused with warmth for the vulnerable genius, Lanier rang the doorbell of van Dyck's waterfront studio. He was expecting a warm welcome, but nothing like this. The diminutive artist, dressed in his painting clothes and splattered with paint, launched himself at Lanier, wrapping his arms round him.

'My dear Nicholas. How are you? How are you?' van Dyck went trilling and gushing on in French, tears in his eyes. 'Oh, how lovely to see you here. And how is dear

Endymion? I shall never forget what you two did for me. Such kindness. Such munificence.'

Lanier smiled fondly as the artist clung to him in coiled embrace. Had they done so much? He and Endymion? Lanier was touched that it had meant so much to him, all those years ago.

In 1620, the Mortlake Tapestry factory had just been opened. It was James's finest achievement as king, by far. James had brought the young van Dyck over to work on tapestry designs, but it was expected that this young up-and-coming artist of massive promise would succeed the royal portrait painter, another Fleming, a plodder called Paul van Somer.

At first all had gone well, largely because van Dyck hardly saw James. He had happy memories of painting Buckingham and his dear wife, Katherine, as Adonis and Venus. Buckingham's fine physique was barely covered by blue drapery. Katherine, in the fashion of the time, was bare-breasted, pouting sweetly above the orange drapery wound round her lower body.

Van Dyck had realised with a thrill of pleasure that this portrait freed him from the sculptural figures of Rubens. Not that he would ever be less than grateful to Rubens the man, as opposed to Rubens the artist.

He had worked in Rubens's studio but not as an apprentice. He had been painting masterpieces since he was fourteen – a stunning self-portrait looking into a mirror. And he had learned anything he had to learn from his master Hendrick van Balen in the elegant Lange Nieuwstraat, in his beloved Antwerp. By the time Rubens took him he was as finished and accomplished as the copies he was set to work producing.

These copies were passed to the engravers, whose work formed an important part of Rubens's income. Rubens needed them executed speedily and efficiently. They were.

Van Dyck, arms flapping, was forever in motion, not so much moving as dashing, even when he painted.

Rubens knew this young man was a great artist from day one at his studio. He knew he was a better painter than he, Rubens, was or ever would be. His reaction to that was to help van Dyck, where he could. Van Dyck was a beneficiary of Rubens's supreme and largely justified self-confidence. He recommended van Dyck to the court of James I of England, partly to help him, partly to remove a potential rival from Rubens's own purlieu. It was an elegant, diplomatic move, typical of Rubens.

Shy and lost, van Dyck arrived in London. Nicholas Lanier was used to welcoming musicians from abroad, with his Huguenot heritage skin deep a generation away he understood how they felt as foreigners. He automatically extended the same welcoming hospitality to van Dyck.

As to Endymion, he was already on the foothills of a lifetime of patronage, mainly to poets and playwrights. He cherished and protected creators in their acts of creation. They all tucked in the lee of his man-mountain presence, shielding them from storms.

It was of great help to van Dyck that Lanier and Endymion spoke excellent French. Van Dyck could speak his native Flemish to the Dutchman, van der Doort, but the lugubrious, sad Surveyor of the King's Pictures had little to say and less desire to say it. He complained of his lot, carried out his duties, then went home.

Van Dyck spoke halting, heavily accented, broken English. This turned out to be the first cause of the agonies he suffered at the hands of James, and almost certainly the reason he never really mastered the language in later life. His mistakes in English and his thick Flemish accent were mocked by James who gave him the nickname Vangoose – a mocking play on his name.

It is just possible that van Dyck's over-awareness of the competition – not only Paul van Somer who had been there for four years, but Hendrick van Steenwijk, Abraham van Blijenberch and above all the more established Daniel Mytens – made him appear hubristic in his gauche self-praise.

But that was quickly slapped out of him, with something even worse than mockery taking its place: James presented a terrifying figure to van Dyck. His eyes rolled lasciviously at any stranger, implicitly inviting the debaucheries taking place all the time in Whitehall.

His tongue was too large for his mouth, van Dyck noticed, with some interest. This resulted in the dribbling of the small beer and wine he constantly consumed. It also meant van Dyck could not understand a word he said.

He neither washed nor changed his clothes, which meant he reeked more than any man the painter had ever met. His straggly red beard was matted with filth, some of which went into his mouth when he ate. He used the weakness in his bowed legs to hang onto the shoulders of any man in the room, his fingers fiddling with his codpiece.

And it did not stop there. Van Dyck was promptly awarded a generous pension, as James assumed he would stay. But it was made graphically clear to van Dyck that in exchange he was expected to become a favourite. The payment was £100. For this £100, the favourite would be expected to consent and submit to any depravities James wished to commit on his person.

This was a soul-shaking shock to van Dyck, not only emotionally but intellectually. He had been brought up on Castiglione's *Book of the Courtier*, often quoting the section about children of noble birth in ancient Greece learning painting as a worthy and necessary accomplishment. He recoiled from the shock of the artist and therefore art being degraded in this way.

His response was a drawing of James in black and red chalk on paper, with white highlighting. James has haunted, hunted eyes, as much a victim of his own lusts as the favourites he preyed on. He is square jawed, but his determination, as well as his learned intelligence, have been swamped by debauchery. James laid bare was a terrible and brilliant sketch of a man out of control.

The sketch was never developed into a portrait of James, because van Dyck had fled the court before there was time to complete the painting. But there was the strangest of ripostes as a kind of companion piece to the sketch. In his 1621 self-portrait, van Dyck goes as far as he dares in painting himself as a female. He shows himself with long rolled hair, eyes just opening wide, pursed red lips and suggestive fingers. It is as if he is saying to James, 'Is this what you desire? Do you see this in me?'

He faced it, quite bravely, then could not face it any more.

In tears, he appealed to Lanier for help. Lanier consulted Endymion. Endymion saved him: van Dyck needed a passport to leave the country. There was a ready excuse to go. There was violent anti-Catholic feeling in London at this time. Van Dyck was denounced by name in Puritan pulpits, by the Bishop of London among others. At the same time, a truce with Spain was about to expire in the Spanish Netherlands. War there was imminent. Van Dyck would be an enemy citizen trapped in London.

Endymion drew on all his compassion, skill and tact to save the painter. He did not appeal for help to Buckingham, in case that provoked James to turn against Buckingham. He would not take that risk to his master. Instead, Endymion fished in the calmer waters of the other great art collector, the Earl of Arundel.

Arundel jumped at the chance of helping the great artist. He issued a 'pass to travel' for eight months. Van Dyck clutched it gratefully and fled back to Antwerp. At that time, he would have said rather hell on hot coals than a return to London. But at that time he did not know James had only four more years to live, to be succeeded by the greatest collector, connoisseur and art patron in Europe.

In his spacious but chaotically cluttered studio, van Dyck introduced his two assistants, Jan van Belcamp and Remigius van Leemput. They bowed politely but not obsequiously to the courtier from England then went about their business.

Charles had allowed Lanier to stay in Antwerp for up to a week while van Dyck painted his portrait. As that week opened before them there was an air of anticipatory targeted bustle, not unlike that outside the studio as the burghers of Antwerp went about their trade with all the known world.

Lanier was curious about van Dyck's surroundings and methods, not having had the chance to witness the painter in action when he was in London. Although he would always be mainly a musician, Lanier was a skilled painter, too. He was humbly ready to learn, as an artist. He had seen enough of van Dyck's work to understand that when you looked at a van Dyck you saw what it was to *be* that man or woman in the painting, to live the life they lived.

On the first day allocated to painting the portrait of Nicholas Lanier, the court clothes Lanier had sent ahead were brought in by Remigius van Leemput, the junior of the two assistants. Van Dyck was obviously familiar with them and had them hung up near a stone slab next to the easel where the pigments bought from an apothecary would later be ground.

Then came The Hour, the crucial hour of posing the sitter. This concentrated hour would be copied by many of van Dyck's successors, notably Lely, as if copying the method might somehow transfer the genius. It did not.

A fascinated, mesmerised, Nicholas Lanier experienced his first Hour. Outwardly, what happened was that van Dyck entered a kind of trance during which he arranged the sitter in a chosen posture. The chosen posture was the external representation of the essence, the very soul of the sitter. It summed the sitter's life so far then illuminated it in light with shape.

Van Dyck had taken on and absorbed the sitter's soul to do this. He was a chameleon who changed with his surroundings and with the company he was in. This quality was purified during The Hour when he became the person he was painting. The only characteristic of himself he retained was his painting talent. At the end of each Hour he was exhausted to the point of collapse.

That was the magic, then came the technique that made it visible. Within the last fifteen minutes of the hour he transferred this posture to one of many little pieces of blue paper, usually squared to make copying easier.

With van Dyck and the sitter watching, the senior assistant, Jan van Belcamp, laid out the pose from the small blue paper to a full-sized sketch on paper, using light chalk strokes. The light chalk strokes reflecting the work-in-progress nature of the sketch.

In that first sitting in Antwerp, Nicholas Lanier's right hand was extended, holding a glove, a symbol of prosperity. But in the finished painting, Lanier's right hand rests on his hip. This associates his success less with money, more to innate nobility. This transformative ability is emphasised in the finished portrait by unusual amounts of white, making Lanier shine, even glow.

Belcamp would paint Lanier's clothes in the pose selected over the coming week.

Meanwhile, van Dyck would paint the face, giving it life. Last of all, one of the assistants would paint in the background according to van Dyck's instructions.

Lanier was not allowed to watch the portrait come to life as he sat in pose that week. Van Dyck occasionally talked to him, but in a distracted, distanced way, as if he had died and gone to heaven. Lanier gave short, courteous replies, assuring the painter he did not need attention.

And then the moment. Nicholas Lanier was allowed to look at his portrait. The assistants were banished. Van Dyck was biting his nails, shaking from shoulders to knees with fear. Lanier looked.

First the outward manifestation. Here was Nicholas Lanier in his prime, in a black cloak tossed with casual elegance over his shoulder; a white silk doublet with puffed sleeves, just short of foppish, slashed to reveal the orange lining. His left hand is leaning, fingers splayed, on the hilt of his sword. The right hand is high on the hip, so the elbow almost forms a right-angle to the body in a classic sprezzatura pose.

This pose, artificial, affected, mannered, is so much part of the cavalier ideal that Castiglione describes it in *The Book of the Courtier*. It indicates nonchalance, succeeding by virtue of being born to success, achieving what is difficult without apparent, or even real, effort. The pose illuminated an attitude to life which led to a way of life expressed in art and literature.

By painting Lanier in this pose van Dyck was paying him a compliment. Lanier was an artisan, an employee, albeit a lofty one as Master of the King's Music. By using a pose often adopted at the Stuart court, a pose he would before long paint the king himself in, van Dyck was exalting his dear friend, the recipient of the painter's considerable warmth.

As to the face, Lanier by van Dyck is cool, self-possessed, slightly sardonic. The direct gaze shows a confidence not found in the preliminary sketch, which has Lanier looking slightly to the left. The face, but especially the eyes, show exquisite sensitivity and refinement. His elegant beard and moustache are in the style of Charles Stuart's. The end of the brush had been used to model the moustache. It was superbly done.

However, there were two things obviously wrong with the painting: The stylised Arcadian background consisted of a vaguely outlined sky in one corner and dark craggy rocks to emphasise the face. But at the bottom left of the painting there was a dead area of failed landscape. Jan van Belcamp had been rushed and it showed.

More seriously, there was a gap between van Dyck's work on the head and van Belcamp's work on the clothes Lanier had sent. There was a line beneath the neck, as if Lanier's head was floating independently of his body.

But somehow it did not matter. In an exercise of genius beyond purpose, van Dyck had created an effect he was unaware of himself. Lanier floating, helped by the touches of white, was reaching for the sublime sky in music and in art.

Lanier in the flesh embraced the tiny Fleming, who was still shaking with emotion and exhaustion.

'I'll take the painting with me,' he said. 'Come to London. His Majesty will be delighted to have you as his court painter.'

Van Dyck nodded, tears streaming down his face. 'Alright.'

# CHAPTER 28
## DAMAGE AND REPAIR

The paintings and sculptures were taken out of the Antwerp warehouse and loaded into carts and carriages. Then Lanier set off overland for London with them. Meanwhile, the treasures loaded aboard the *Margaret* to be sent by sea arrived in England. Endymion arranged for them to be unpacked in the Banqueting House at Whitehall, accompanied only by Abraham van der Doort.

The Dutchman's bitterness was growing like a cancer. He was an engraver who wanted to be an artist as his brothers were. But the talent did not reach the aspiration. And in any case the local London painters had shut him out of the market.

The London Company of Painters and Stainers had got up a petition against all foreign artists with Muytens and van der Doort specified by name. If they wished to stay painters they had to live beyond the City walls. Muytens complied. For van der Doort living beyond the City walls would make his court role as Surveyor of the King's Pictures near impossible. He decided not to push his ordinary talents any further and gave up painting.

He had arrived at Henry's court nearly twenty years ago and became the keeper of Henry's cabinet. This clerking job offered him a surprising measure of fulfilment as he worshipped Henry, all he stood for and all he would become. The young prince's death was yet another hammer-blow from life. Van der Doort made part of Henry's wax funeral effigy. His own life froze into wax with it.

He needed his recent appointment as Surveyor of the King's Pictures for Charles but hated the work. Even aside from Charles's daily interferences, van der Doort spoke broken English with a heavy Dutch accent and had never learned to write English, which it was his job to do.

Also, he was required to list information he often did not have about the item's provenance, size and value. He was expected to know in which of the many galleries in the many palaces it was hanging. Any mistakes he made would be pounced on with unforgiving prissy precision. Charles and his annotations hung like a permanent black cloud over the battered Dutchman.

Abraham van der Doort looked at the crates full of art from the *Margaret* and groaned. He felt full of bile at the sight of them. Endless cataloguing beckoned. Bone-deep gloom settled over him.

'What's he going to do with all this lot? Eh?'

Endymion squeezed his arm encouragingly. He powerfully crowbarred open the first crate of paintings on the spacious floor of the Banqueting House. Van der Doort's gloom quickly turned to alarm. Endymion was horrified.

Many of the paintings were merely frames round black canvas. Tickets indicated Raphael's *Madonna*, Titian's *Twelve Caesars*, *The Three Graces* by Guido Reni and *St Jerome* by Guilio Romano. But all were black with no painting visible. Aghast, Endymion and van der Doort stopped looking at the damage.

Van der Doort's mouth was wide open. He stared blankly at Endymion. 'What happened?'

Endymion was pale. 'I'm not sure. It could be mercury. If there was mercury stored in the hold of the ship and there was a storm. That would turn the paintings black.'

'Can we do something for it? His Majesty will blame me. He always blame me.'

Endymion ignored that. 'Possibly. Possibly it can be reversed. We need to get all the damaged paintings over to William Peake's shop in the Strand. He can fix them if anyone can, along with Faithorne and Dobson. They are miracle workers at restoration.'

'They will need to be.'

All three Williams – Peake, Faithorne and Dobson – were gathered round the blackened masterpieces from the Gonzaga collection, spoiled aboard the *Margaret*. Endymion towered over them. Van der Doort had gone back to his dismal room in Broad Street ward.

'It's mercury alright,' William Peake said. 'But this is outside my competence. There are two men in London who could solve this one for you, Endymion. One is Theodore Mayerne, who has the knowledge but is too eminent to approach. The other is Jerome Lanier.'

'I'm not familiar with him,' Endymion said. 'A relation of Nicholas's presumably?'

'He is Nicholas's uncle. That is fortunate. He will likely be keen to avoid the opprobrium that will be heaped on his nephew if it can be shown the paintings were not stored properly.'

'Unfair, but true,' Faithorne the engraver said.

Dobson belched. He was dark haired, medium height and build with a raffish manner. He was drunk, mid-afternoon, but holding it well. 'Is this Jerome Lanier the sackbut player? He's one of the King's Musicians, isn't he? I've heard him play.'

'Oh, you do get around, Dobson, don't you?' Faithorne said. 'Here there and everywhere. Bloody ubiquitous.'

Dobson grinned.

A link-boy was sent to Jerome Lanier with a note. As Peake had forecast, he came immediately on learning of his nephew's involvement. There was so far no talk of payment for his services. Jerome resembled his nephew in his clear-cut Huguenot good looks. He was an amateur artist of some ability and a noted collector, with an especially good eye for the French art of his heritage.

'It's quicksilver alright,' Jerome said as soon as he saw the paintings. 'Mercury, that is. Nicholas told me there had been a storm in the Gulf of Venice. He feared all may have been lost. The mercury was probably stored as medicine.

Badly stored. Keep that under your hat, though, or Nicholas could be in trouble.'

'Of course I will,' Endymion said. 'How is Nicholas?'

'Happy but poor. Elizabeth, his wife, has petitioned His Majesty for £200 towards all the money he was owed from his time in Mantua.'

Endymion Porter, ever the courtier and diplomat, changed the subject. 'Can you do anything?' He nodded at the pictures.

'I can try.' Jerome looked thoughtful. 'Look, Endymion, why don't you scoot off, eh? No point in making a spectator sport of it. I'll send word as and when.'

Endymion nodded ponderously. 'Fair enough. Good luck.'

Watched by the three Williams, Jerome Lanier used spittle mixed with warm milk, rubbing the mixture gently into the paintings with cotton buds. It was clearly beginning to work, albeit slowly and imperfectly.

'Try aqua vitae,' William Dobson said. He opened his eyes to say it. He seemed to have been asleep standing up.

Jerome Lanier threw him a quizzical look, reluctantly impressed.

The aqua vitae took off the more recalcitrant black spots. Jerome Lanier increased the strength, letting the ethyl alcohol seep into the pigment. Some of the greatest paintings of the age began to come to life before their eyes.

The three Williams and Jerome Lanier kept at it for hours. They had lanterns brought, and tapers for close work. They experimented with the strength of the aqua vitae, occasionally mixing it with spittle.

'I can restore them from here,' Dobson said. 'All of them. Let me try, at least.' He was sober now.

'We'll see what Endymion says,' William Peake said. He paused. 'But I think you can do it, William. I'll tell Endymion that.'

In the end, some of the most precious damaged paintings were sent back to van Dyck to partially repaint, as his first task as court painter, before he had even left Antwerp. Titian's *Galba* was one of these. But Rubens's *Vitellius* was irredeemably damaged. Van Dyck ran up a replacement copy for a fee of £20.

William Dobson restored and retouched *The Three Graces* by Guido Reni and St Jerome by Guilio Romano, among others. They were sent to van Dyck to see if he could make any further improvements. He could not. But he sent back a letter by return asking William Dobson to become his assistant when he arrived in London.

# CHAPTER 29
## BUCKINGHAM'S WAR

Charles and Henrietta were locked in the Privy Rooms at Whitehall, inside concentric layers of other rooms, like snails in layers of shell. Both yearned for the success of Buckingham's expedition to La Rochelle, though Henrietta cherished the secret hope that Buckingham would die – gloriously, naturally, – in the attempt, so Charles would belong solely to her.

If anything, Henrietta's passion for the expedition's success was even greater than Charles's. Parliament assumed that because the English were fighting her brother, Louis, Henrietta's heart was with the Catholic forces. Nothing could have been further from the truth.

Henrietta was a woman of violent loves and violent hates; she hated Richelieu with a passion. The Huguenot uprising against Louis started when Richelieu came to power. The Huguenots feared that any cardinal, let alone a *dévot* like Richelieu, would raise an army against them.

Their worst fears were realised when Richelieu did indeed start to raise an army, ostensibly for service in Germany, but the Huguenots of La Rochelle feared it would be used against them. So did Buckingham.

There was another reason Parliament's suspicions of Henrietta were misplaced. Henrietta was indifferent to the brother the English were fighting against, Louis. The brother she loved, dear Gaston, now Duke of Orleans, was allied with Buckingham as part of an emerging new Protestant alliance. Although like the other small states in the alliance, Gaston would only send troops once Buckingham had taken La Rochelle.

The dream from Henry and Frederick's time of the scattered Protestant states uniting against the giant Catholic powers had been awakened again. The people of

England had been told the attack on La Rochelle would create a Protestant union to rescue and restore Elizabeth and Frederick, the old dream.

Charles had sent his close friend from the Spanish trip, Wat Montagu, to negotiate with the Protestant states in France, to stiffen their resolve. That had been Henrietta's idea. She had every faith in 'pretty little Wat Montagu' and his excellent French.

Montagu was promptly captured by Richelieu's agents with all the correspondence with the French Protestant kingdoms still about his person.

Charles threw himself into the rescue of the Huguenots of La Rochelle. Buckingham insisted on commanding the English fleet himself, even though Katherine and his mother begged him on their knees not to. He was, he reminded them, the Admiral of the Fleet. The trouble was, there was no English fleet, or hardly one worthy of the name. It had lapsed into desuetude since its glory days under Queen Elizabeth

The ever devoted Phineas Pett, the King's Master Shipwright, put himself totally at the king's service, despite being crushed by his wife and his only sister having died in the same month last winter.

The navy had been run to ruin by Buckingham's predecessor as Admiral of the Fleet, Charles Howard, Duke of Nottingham. There were only forty-three ships afloat and seaworthy, a fraction of the naval might that set sail under Gloriana.

Pett stopped all other work at the Poplar Shipyards. Working by day and by lamplight at night, he drove the building of ten small vessels, just 120 tons each, with a single deck and a quarter deck only. They could be rowed as well as sailed, so they would be suitable for the shallow waters around La Rochelle. Equally important, they would be suitable for the even shallower waters round the islands which guarded the port, principally the fortified island of Île de Ré.

But there was no money to pay for the construction of these Lion's Whelps, as the ships became known. Parliament, as ever, approved the policy of attacking Louis's forces and defending the Huguenots at La Rochelle, but refused to vote for the money to pay for it.

Richard Weston, the Chancellor of the Exchequer, attended petulant meetings with Charles. He brought along his lugubrious secretary, John Gibbons, who irritated Charles by taking ages to look in musty ledgers then emerging from them, blinking like a mole, to tell him he had not got any money at all, let alone the £200,000 or so he needed to make war.

Charles would have to find new money, presumably via taxes. To his surprise, Weston did not make any fuss about the obvious solution. This was to extend the navy tax, Ship Money, to the citizens of inland cities. As an afterthought, they levied what amounted to forced loans on the nobles, via local justices of the peace.

Charles never noticed the state of abject terror he invoked in his Lord Chancellor, nor Weston's quite deliberate use of the mouldering clerk Gibbons as a living delaying tactic.

Buckingham waded in; money was needed, Buckingham would find it. He moved out of York House and found a tenant for it, to raise money for the expedition. He made sure the tenant – Francis Manners, sixth Earl of Rutland, a kinsman of Katherine's – was an art lover who would cherish the paintings and sculptures at York House.

He sold a large quantity of his jewels and jewellery, using Diego Duarte who was very active as the king's jeweller and an experienced raiser of money for the royal purse.

Every spare farthing Buckingham had was put toward the expedition. And he was not the only one. The Victualler of the Navy, Sir Alan Apsley, put £5000 of his own money toward the expedition. All ranking naval personnel were encouraged to contribute by a forceful Buckingham.

Buckingham turned into a charging bull. He was exchanging insulting letters with Richelieu, who he hoped to bring down soon, using the nascent Protestant alliance. He dreamed incessantly that his coming defeat of Louis would enable him to possess Anne of Austria again. The long dreamed of Protestant alliance had never seemed nearer. The rescue of Montague from Richelieu's captivity was in the tangled skein of his dreams somewhere, but that was a lesser matter.

The first task was to design his costume as commander. The costume, he wrote to Katherine, who was back at New Hall, their mansion in Essex, boasted 'an immense collar and a magnificent plume of feathers in the hat'. He also designed a uniform for his elite men, specifying the swords, daggers and pistols to go with it. But in the end there was no time to have the jackets run up and the weapons bought.

Next, he had to decide what to take with him on the high seas, into battle. A large collier ship was stocked with fine food and the best wine. He took most of his unsold jewels with him, along with furniture, books and his most ornate carriage, with saddle horses to draw it.

He took a trip to Mortlake to select tapestries for his cabin aboard his flagship. He selected a *Death of Scipio* with Francis Cleyn's beautiful gold and silver embroidered edges. He also took Francis Cleyn's *Venus and Vulcan*. Both of these tapestries had been commissioned from Cleyn by Buckingham, though they were kept at Mortlake.

Buckingham's trip to Mortlake was one of the few times he incurred Henrietta's approval. Mortlake, as she frequently reminded Charles, was inspired by, if not copied from, her father's tapestry works set up in Paris in 1607.

The expedition was nearly ready. Buckingham planned a huge farewell dinner and masque for Charles and Henrietta, at Whitehall. He commissioned James Shirley to write an allegory in which he played the chief part, as both Fame and Truth. After him came Envy represented by dancers in dog's heads representing the people barking. Nearly a hundred nobles participated in the dance.

Charles and Henrietta danced with a will at the post-masque dance, though they took no part in the masque itself. Charles had his hair all *gaufré* and frizzled. He was wearing the same clothes he wore for his portrait by Daniel Mytens, a pointed waistline and sloping shoulders with epaulettes, all carefully sewn to make his body look straighter than it was.

Two days later, Charles travelled to Portsmouth alone for a farewell dinner with Buckingham aboard his flagship. Charles loved the salt air and cobblestones of Portsmouth. He loved the navy, he loved ships. He was proud of his knowledge of maritime matters and tended to flaunt it. The *Triumph*, he told Buckingham and the ship's captain, Sir John Watts, 'is a little too hard in her helm'. Buckingham and Watts solemnly nodded at the truth of this.

Next morning, Buckingham set sail with a hundred ships, eight thousand infantry and one thousand cavalry. The fleet looked imposing as it sailed into the distance, but Charles was unaware of the underlying ragged state of the flotilla as it headed for La Rochelle.

Despite Phineas Pett's best efforts most of the ships were rotting. Sir Alan Apsley, the Victualler, had been completely unable to stop the pursers selling off most of the food privately then pocketing the proceeds, leaving the sailors hungry. Many of the ragamuffin crews had no boots. They had not been paid for as long as anybody could remember, neither had the soldiers.

The majority of them had been pressganged in the first place, often after violent fights with their captors. They had been at the point of mutiny for some time, desertions had been rife. Wild groups of them, including some captains, had already forced their way into Whitehall, where they were beaten back by Charles's bodyguards.

They had then attacked York House, where they found Buckingham absent and bewildered tenants in place. Then on to the Admiralty, where they threatened to pull down the house of the Paymaster, Sir William Russell, unless he found some money for them.

Wat Montagu had been seized by Richelieu's agents on his way back from a meeting with Gaston, Duke of Orleans, who had solemnly promised help for the Protestant coalition of the moment. La Rochelle was captured by Buckingham, but not before Richelieu's men took Montagu to Paris. He was imprisoned in the Bastille, but treated well, given good food and allowed any books he wanted. Many of the books he requested were of Catholic theology to deepen his knowledge before taking vows in the Catholic priesthood.

This endeared him to Richelieu who became a frequent visitor. He was also received by Louis at the Louvre. Montagu told him that Buckingham was the thorn in the flesh in Anglo-French relations, once plucked the two countries were natural allies. Louis did not disagree but Buckingham's continuing passion for his wife, by now a very open secret, allowed no compromise.

With Montagu a hostage, Richelieu used his advantage to put more pressure on Henrietta. He insisted she agitate for the removal of penalties on all Catholics who practised their religion in private. This she did. With his usual flair for theatre, Richelieu then demanded that Henrietta walk barefoot to Tyburn to honour the Catholics martyred there for their religion. Charles agreed she had little option but to comply with this public display of faith, but he made it a clear condition for Montagu's release.

Montagu was given a private message by Richelieu before he left the Bastille. It was not only unwritten it was almost unsaid, being whispered into his ear on Richelieu's sweetest sultana-scented outbreath. The message was for Buckingham. It was that Richelieu intended to have him killed for dishonouring the French queen.

Two of the finest talents of their generation stood up to their calves in the water slopping through the gun ports aboard Buckingham's flagship, the *Triumph*. In the distance, they could hear cannon fire though, perhaps fortunately, not the cries and screams of their own soldiers.

Ostensibly, the two men had little in common. One was Dutch one was English. The Dutchman was more than twenty years older and of a mechanical turn of mind. The Englishman was so much the poet he spoke and dreamed in rhythm and rhyme.

They were both attached to the court of King Charles – they had that at least in common. But what united them, bound them together tighter than many brothers, was a common need. The need was to keep their utter misery hidden behind a mask of duty willingly, even thankfully, carried out.

Robert Herrick felt closer to Cornelis Drebbel than to any other man on the ship. Even closer than to a fellow poet, well-known to him from London, who was also on board. This was the bred-inn-the-bone royalist, the nineteen-year-old John Suckling, fresh out of Cambridge, who had put his slight frame at his monarch's disposal.

Herrick and Drebbel it was, then. Together and united. The Englishman's story was the simpler of the two. Charles Stuart was the patron of many poets. His lessons with Henry Peacham had taught him that the Athens of Pericles regarded the production of plays and poetry as a public service. As soon as he was crowned, nearly three years ago, he made the patronage of poets a priority.

In this he had Henrietta's full support. Henrietta's grandmother was Jeanne d'Albret, a noted poet, who had produced truly original work in a sort of demotic medieval

French. Jeanne had converted to Protestantism, as her son, Henrietta's father, Henri IV, was later to do. Indeed, it was Henri who gave La Rochelle to the Huguenots, as a place of safety.

By a strange quirk of fate, Jeanne herself had washed up at La Rochelle. For a while, she led the Huguenot resistance to Catholic forces trying to take the city. It would have appealed to Herrick's wry, ironic nature if he had known that the spirit of the Catholic Henrietta's grandmother stood with him in the fight against the present-day Catholics.

As Henrietta was quick to point out when she first met Herrick, not only her famous grandmother but her father also wrote poetry: 'My father once said, "I would rather the expenditures for my table were curtailed in order that men of letters may be amply remunerated," she told the poet, who nodded approvingly.

She then told him her favourite story about her father, the story of his patronage of Ronsard, that she had told Charles at their first meeting.

'Admirable,' said Herrick, dryly, hoping a similar benison might fall to him as to the fortunate Ronsard.

Charles's patronage of Herrick, however, turned out to be neither a forest, as Henri had given Ronsard, nor, disappointingly, money. Herrick was appointed first to the royal chapel at Whitehall, then to the living at the vicarage at Dean Prior on Dartmoor in the diocese of Exeter.

He had lived there for a year as priest and was about to be confirmed in the living when he was ordered away to minister to this damned expedition. That was how he habitually referred, sotto voce to Drebbel, to the rescue of the Huguenots at La Rochelle which had left them both up to their calves in sea water aboard a leaking ship.

Herrick hated being a priest; religion had so much of pretence about it. He had no calling and no particular knowledge of or interest in the scriptures. He needed the stipend, though, to write poetry all day.

During what he wrote to Endymion was 'a long and irksome banishment' in the wilds of Dartmoor, he was working on a hymn to pastoral innocence, a long series of poems called *Hesperides* – a reference to the Garden of Hesperus, a mythological place of retreat.

In this series, lads and lasses play at their rural pastimes. Herrick would sing of brooks, of blossoms, and bowers. But inspiration came slowly, not least because he hated actually dwelling in the rural idyll that was so beautiful as an abstract ideal.

Cornelis Drebbel's story reached back further and was more tangled. He was from Alkmaar in the Netherlands and had a background in alchemy and engraving. His brother-in-law was the court engraver, Hendrick Goltzius.

Charles felt as if he had grown up with the knobbly Dutchman who looked like a Dutch farmer, always cheaply dressed in black, all wild hair, potato nose and homely, ruddy face. Drebbel had invented the camera obscura, his fame would surely last forever for that. But there was an even greater wonder.

Charles was seven when Drebbel, attached to Henry's court, demonstrated a perpetuum mobile machine he had constructed. The perpetuum mobile showed liquid in a glass tube which rose and fell in a manner resembling the sea. Amazingly, it did not stop moving.

Perpetual motion. Was it magic or mechanics? The hand of God or the hand of man? It started Charles's lifelong fascination with movement and motion. Movement in an apparently still painting; movement in the masque and in the anti-masque; dance as beautiful movement, still less painful for him than walking with two feet flat to the ground.

There was no mysticism in Drebbel's machine, not to Charles. He never really believed in a higher power behind or beyond beauty, though he had to pretend to. It was an air barometer with a clock mechanism attached; the motion was caused by the changes in atmospheric pressure. It was explicable.

To Charles's delight the principles behind the system represented a return to the old Ptolemaic system against the new Copernician. It was looking back not forward. How Charles approved of that. The return to the rural idyll was also looking back, going back where we were before the monster city imposed itself.

The perpetuum mobile was adapted to work in clocks. Drebbel designed other automata for use in masques, assisting Inigo with stage design and construction. Charles watched all this with fascination. He was delighted to appoint Drebbel to his court after his coronation.

Elizabeth and Frederick applauded Drebbel's rise, too. He had been at Prague, at the court, during their all too brief reign in Bohemia. In a letter to Charles, Elizabeth remembered a clavichord Drebbel had constructed which played by the rays of the sun. Brother and sister were at one in their admiration for the Dutchman's ingenuity.

But now, Drebbel feared, his fortunes may have taken a turn for the worse. Charles and Phineas Pett had put Drebbel's remarkable skills as an inventor at the service of the navy. He had been given a workshop and dwelling house in the Minories, between Aldgate and the Tower of London.

Here, Drebbel's wild imagination ran riot, much to Charles's wide-eyed delight. He constructed a submarine, a ship that would function fully underwater. He demonstrated its efficacy under the Thames.

Among the weapons he designed were water-mines and water petards. He turned his knowledge of pyrotechnics, also used for the masques, toward producing explosives which were to be directed against French fortifications at La Rochelle.

However, the problem was, to Drebbel's increasing concern, that none of his inventions were working successfully. Only yesterday, Buckingham's forces had tried to set fire to the French fleet with Drebbel's floating petards.

The body of these petards was made of iron filled with gunpowder. This floated on a piece of willow. A spring was placed through the willow to activate the gunpowder when it encounters the hull of the ship. Which it did, but the effect was not to blow the fifteen or sixteen foot hole in the ship as calculated, but to blow water into the air.

All Drebbel's other maritime inventions were similarly unsuccessful. The sailors, unpaid, hungry and inadequately armed, were turning against him. Herrick had started loudly praying as soon as hostile groups of them approached Drebbel, indignant at the latest failure, in an effort to ward off attacks on the Dutchman.

# CHAPTER 31
## DEATH WILL COME AND MAR THE SONG

Even at anchor, even on a placid July day under a cerulean blue sky with fluffy clouds, the *Triumph* was heaving. Robert Herrick's gaze sought land. It alighted, pleading for relief, on the distant, twisting shape of the Île de Ré, looking like a serpent basking in the placid waters of the bay, the Pertuis Breton.

The poet was suffering mightily, voiding any food which briefly reached his stomach. Cornelis Drebbel was largely unaffected by the motion beneath his feet, being absorbed still by the successive failure of his devices. The blonde, waif-like John Suckling was regaling the other two with the story of Buckingham's latest diplomatic scrapes.

As an isolated Protestant enclave, La Rochelle had been attacked many times before by overwhelming numbers of the Catholic majority in France. On the last occasion, three years ago, the people of La Rochelle had appealed for help to two of the Protestant alliance, the Count of Soubise and his brother, the Duke of Rohan.

Soubise had appeared again, in La Rochelle's hour of need, in charge of its defence. He had met Buckingham at La Rochelle last night, John Suckling reported to Herrick and Drebbel. There had been a spectacular falling out, something Buckingham was prone to during any contact, diplomatic or otherwise.

Soubise had not wanted Buckingham's forces to enter La Rochelle at all, as he had not given up hope of a rapprochement with Louis. The French king, inspired by the fox-like red eminence, Richelieu, had dangled compromise just as the bellicose English arrived.

Buckingham had lost his head, Suckling said, lost his temper, lost his dignity. He insulted Soubise. What, he demanded finally was he supposed to do, having come all this way, if he was not even allowed into the city he was supposed to be defending?

Soubise had an answer for that. The English should attack the heavily defended forts around La Rochelle first, starting with the Île de Ré. So, as Suckling understood it, the English force which was in such a state it had barely made the journey, was now to capture a heavily defended fort with unpaid hungry and untrained forces.

'But we shall bear arms according to the discipline and practice of cavaliers!' declared Suckling, optimistically.

Herrick had had enough of all this. Fighting was fighting, he did not care for the details. He retreated into his own world, where he was happiest.

'I have written a poem,' he croaked out, hoarsely. 'It is to my dear patron, Endymion Porter.'

Although Charles was nominally Herrick's patron, it was Endymion's money which actually paid him. Suckling, who was one of a number of poets and playwrights also sponsored by Endymion, clapped enthusiastically.

Steadying himself against the swaying of the ship at anchor, Herrick adopted a declamatory stance and declaimed his poem, booming with heavy emphasis to reflect the mock heroic style of the verse:

> *Let there be patrons, patrons like to thee,*
> *Brave Porter! poets ne'er will wanting be:*
> *Fabius and Cotta, Lentulus, all live*
> *In thee, thou man of men! who here do'st give*
> *Not only subject-matter for our wit,*
> *But likewise oil of maintenance to it.*

Suckling renewed delighted clapping, shaking his slight frame. Herrick took a mock bow.

Drebbel smiled wanly. He had not been listening. Instead, he was picturing the plans of his floating petard in his mind. The gunpowder was exploding too early. But why? Why? Why?

As Drebbel disappeared back into the realms of mechanical theory, the two poets drew together as wind whipped round them on deck, as if comforting each other in the massive comfort of Endymion Porter's embrace.

'How is work progressing on the walled garden, outside time?' Suckling asked. He meant the *Hesperides* cycle.

'I think it will run to over a thousand poems,' Herrick muttered, gloomily. 'It shows no sign of ever coming to a halt. I am currently concerned with the stopping of a transient moment in time, such as in the coming of good luck when one wishes the moment to stop, all motion to cease.'

Drebbel glanced at him with an automatic smile, momentarily interested at that.

Suckling had both heard and read some of the poems and was an artless enthusiast for the older man's work.

'Tell me,' he said. 'Is Anacreon still central to the work? I love his tendency to wry self-mockery. He is a portrait of his creator.'

Herrick gathered himself, fearing he was going to be ill again, despite having eaten nothing for hours. 'I have a piece,' he said. 'It is a lyric to mirth. It is a plea to enjoy our merriment, such as we are experiencing now, voiding the stomach and watching our bedraggled forces throw themselves wildly to their death. Enjoy this moment, I sing, before death comes along and ruins its perfection.'

'Do you have it by heart?' Suckling said. 'Say it to me.'

'Avec plaisir, my boy. Here it is. Well, a verse of it. *A Lyric to Mirth.*

*Rouse Anacreon from the dead,*
*And return him drunk to bed:*
*Sing o'er Horace, for ere long*
*Death will come and mar the song:*

*Then shall Wilson and Gaultier*
*Never sing or play more here.'*

Suckling was grinning, eyes dancing. 'Bravo, bravo! Who are Wilson and Gaultier?'

'Two of the king's musicians. Gaultier is sublime on the lute.'

'I do not approve of fellows like him,' Drebbel pronounced, his attention once more engaged.

Herrick laughed. 'Jacques Gaultier was at the French court,' he told Suckling. 'About ten years ago, he killed a nobleman there and fled, some say with our Lord Buckingham's assistance. His Lordship certainly protected him when the French tried to get him back for trial. Buckingham was tweaking Richelieu's beard, as usual. At any rate, His Majesty put him on the payroll to keep him safe. An annuity of £100, so I am reliably informed.'

Drebbel grimaced at the amount.

'Why did you say you do not approve of him?' Suckling asked Drebbel, sounding boyish even to his own ears. 'Was it the murder of this nobleman?'

Drebbel shrugged, uneasy with the subject. His homely face twisted with distaste. 'No woman is safe in his presence, let alone in his company. He seeks to have his way and ruin them, indiscriminately and with all too much success. His lute playing is put at service of this ignoble quest.'

Herrick laughed at Drebbel's discomfort with the subject of seduction.

The next occasion the three men met on deck, Suckling was spattered with blood. He had apparently acquitted himself well in battle.

The island of Île de Ré, which Buckingham was now committed to attacking, was well-guarded by Fort St Martin, just visible from the deck of Buckingham's anchored flagship. It was a formidable defensive fortification, capable of repulsing even a well-trained army. The star shape of the thick walls increased both the number of surfaces the enemy had to bombard and the amount and angle of returning fire.

Richelieu had sent crack troops to bolster its defence, from the elite Champagne Regiment, nicknamed the Invincibles. They were well supplied with modern ordnance, arms and ammunition and with enough corn, salt-fish and wine to withstand a long siege. The governor of the fort, Jeanne de Caylar d'Anduze de Saint-Bonnet, Marquis of Toiras, had plenty of warning of the English attack. The women and children had been evacuated.

Buckingham rued his own lack of engineers and effective siege-breaking equipment. He had long ago lost faith in Drebbel's various siege engines and petards, none of which worked. St Martin would have to be stormed by brute force with no mechanical aid.

Driven by a strong northerly wind, the English force approached in the shallow-draught Lion's Whelp boats Phineas Pett had thrown together in double time back at the Poplar shipyards. A fascinated but horrified Herrick watched from the deck of the *Triumph*, as the Lion's Whelps tried several times to land. Suckling was in the lead boat. Drebbel had gone below unable to watch.

Eventually, around eight thousand badly equipped Englishmen landed on the beaches. Toiras sent a force out to them, but the English were larger in numbers than he had expected and under a well-organised enfilade fire, the French were driven back to the fort, where they remained.

'Buckingham was lion hearted,' Suckling later reported to Herrick. He left unsaid that a lion heart did not compensate for a total lack of military knowledge or siege tactics.

Buckingham set up camp, waiting far too long before attacking. Disease broke out among the Englishmen in the fetid air of the island's marshland. The English called it 'the bloody flux'. It laid hundreds low, voiding their stomachs by every means in their bodies until they were as weak as mice.

Eventually, the English stormed the fort with Buckingham in the lead, apparently fearless of impending death. Had his siege ladder been long enough he would have scaled the fortress walls at the head of his men, before certain death. But none of the ladders were anywhere near long enough, so Buckingham and the leading Englishmen slid ignominiously down again.

The ignominy did not stop there. The retreating English foot-soldiers, under fusillades of cannon, ambuscade and musket fire from the fort, were trampled by their own cavalry, which Buckingham had inexplicably placed in the rear, instead of at the front.

'I thought this day was my last,' Suckling told Herrick. 'I lay on the soft ground, breathing in marsh fumes, while all around me our men were trampled by our own cavalry in the stinking salt pits. As we floundered against each other, the French attacked from the rear and killed us at will.'

Around three thousand of the eight thousand infantry survived, with about half the cavalry. Thirty-two regimental colours were captured by the enemy that day and more lost. It was the most humiliating defeat since the loss of Normandy. London wits dubbed the Île de Ré the Isle of Rue.

Back in England after the Île de Ré debacle, Buckingham went nowhere without a bodyguard, although he scorned the wearing of a jacket of chain mail, which Charles urged on him.

Not only was he in danger, anybody associated with him was, too. His astrologer and physician, Dr John Lambe, was recognised by a mob in Cheapside as he walked home from the theatre. The mob called after him that he was 'the Duke's devil' – his familiar in witchcraft. They stoned him, chased him, finally beat him to death despite the best efforts of four constables who came to his aid and arrested two of the mob. They were both later released.

Buckingham reacted with gritted-teeth bravura. He nagged Charles at every opportunity for a second attempt to capture Ré and La Rochelle, a second expedition. Charles was wavering, almost convinced.

The idea was reasonable, after all. Or so it seemed to Charles. A huge relief force under Henry Holland had been ready to sail from Portsmouth to Buckingham's aid. It would have reached him in time to provide the force he needed at Île de Ré, had it not been pinned back in port by violent and unusual contrary winds. A malign shift of wind direction had already allowed the French to resupply the St Martin garrison with ordnance during Buckingham's siege.

This double blow from the fates added to Charles's unease that he was destined for an unlucky reign. Henry Holland's fleet was still in port, in Portsmouth, though, which meant the French took the threat of a second attempt seriously. It accelerated and concentrated Richelieu's plans to have Buckingham killed.

Shortly after the defeat at Île de Ré, a large relief force of Richelieu's troops under Marshal Schomberg had arrived at La Rochelle. On Richelieu's orders, Soubise was sent back to Paris accompanied by a discreet force of Richelieu's personal guard. Soubise's falling out with Buckingham was known to Richelieu. He was Richelieu's creature now.

The red Cardinal gave Soubise to understand that he had been chosen to avenge French honour by arranging the end of Buckingham's time on this earth. Soubise was instructed to start interviewing the five hundred English prisoners taken at Île de Ré until he found a suitable assassin. Richelieu told him to look for someone with a personal grievance, the usual bitterness was not enough, as Richelieu instinctively understood.

Soubise found his man on the first day of looking. Lieutenant John Felton was owed years of back pay, a massive £80. He had been passed over for promotion. Stemming from a family of minor Suffolk gentry, his service of king and country had left him ruined, homeless and starving.

Felton felt himself fortunate to be selected for the task in hand, manna from heaven. He seethed and stewed with resentment at Buckingham. He had just watched most of his friends and comrades die miserably because of their commander's idiocy and vanity. Those who had not died Buckingham let starve without their fair dues while he went whoring with French women in his gaudy clothes.

Parliament had just issued a Remonstrance against Buckingham, demanding his removal from all offices, but that was not enough, Felton thought. Soubise made sure John Felton had a copy of the Remonstrance, which had been reprinted as a popular pamphlet by the Puritan press. He would have got hold of one anyway, they were everywhere.

With Richelieu's coins in his purse, the former lieutenant bought a three-edged knife for ten pence at a cutler's shop on Tower Hill. Next day, he used more of the money Soubise had personally handed over to purchase a horse to ride to Portsmouth, there to search out Buckingham.

Charles was staying near Portsmouth so he could the review the fleet which had been gathered for Buckingham's support. Buckingham was hoping to make the fleet ready to sail to victory at La Rochelle. He was staying in Portsmouth High Street, at the Greyhound Inn.

Also at the inn were Soubise, his brother, the Duke of Rohan, and a conclave of others Buckingham hoped might advance the Protestant cause. Buckingham imagined he and Soubise were now reconciled after their spat, as he viewed it. He had spent the previous evening showing Soubise and Rohan the plans Inigo had drawn up to redesign the Strand frontage of York House.

Almost opposite the Greyhound Inn on the cobbled High Street was the Square Tower. Here, Le Seuer's bust of Charles rested, displaying a solid tranquillity in art its object never achieved in life. The bust was of bronze and Charles was wearing his beloved Garter insignia. He had placed similar busts in many of the major towns of the realm.

He greatly approved of this particular bust. He resolved to describe it to Henrietta when he got back to London. He hated the separation from her, but she hoped she might be pregnant and did not wish to travel.

Buckingham's wife, Katherine, was with him, though, along with their baby son. Katherine was nervous of a prophecy by the soothsayer Lady Eleanor Davies, the Earl of Castlehaven's daughter. She said the Duke would die in August in the year 1628. Buckingham told Kate Eleanor Davies had been tried for witchcraft, which was true.

John Felton arrived in Portsmouth on 23 August, 1628. He enquired of the street throng where he could find the Duke of Buckingham.

Although he did not, of course, mention it to Katherine, Buckingham felt the first prickling of fear in the nape of his neck at the same time as Felton passed Le Sueur's statue of Charles. He truly did despise the Eleanor Davies prophecy, but there was something else which troubled him mightily.

Two weeks ago, back in London, Buckingham and Katherine along with Charles and Henrietta had seen a staging of Shakespeare's *Henry VIII* at the Globe, by the King's Players. Henry VIII's Duke of Buckingham had been executed on Tower Hill. In William Shakespeare's play, resounding in Buckingham's head, Norfolk says to Buckingham, 'Be advised. *Heat not a furnace for your foe so hot that it do singe yourself*'.

Had Buckingham done precisely that? His foe was Richelieu. Had he heated the furnace so hot it would singe himself?

More of the playwright's words from Norfolk to his Buckingham rang in Buckingham's head: 'We may outrun by violent swiftness that which we run at. And lose by over-running.' A second expedition to La Rochelle was impossible, wasn't it? It was over-running. It would not happen. Would it?

It was quite early in the morning. There was some sort of disturbance going on in the streets of Portsmouth. John Felton, with assumed conviviality, asked a couple of roughnecks what was going on. There had been a mutiny on the Green yesterday evening, he was told. Some poor seamen had been hanged on a gibbet on the beach. The sailors had had enough. There were mutinies while the ships were still in port.

John Felton made his way into the Greyhound Inn. At that very moment, Buckingham came down, sharp at nine o'clock, to make his toilet before breakfast in a room connected by a dark passage to the central hall. He dressed, accompanied by Soubise, Rohan and others sympathetic to his cause of a return to La Rochelle.

He went out into the central hall. Felton came in the door. He strode forward in blood-blind fury just as Buckingham turned to say something to Soubise. Felton took his knife and plunged it into Buckingham's left breast, deep into the vena cava. Buckingham staggered and choked out 'Villain!' before blood filled his mouth, then spurted out. He convulsively pulled out the knife, then fell to the floor, mortally wounded.

Soubise and Rohan were yelling: 'Seize him! Seize him!' They blocked the way to Felton to such effect that he nearly escaped, but he was held fast until the guard appeared.

Upstairs, Katherine heard the commotion. She instantly knew what had happened. Baby George Villiers, who carried the same name as his father, was asleep in his crib. Katherine was already showing with Buckingham's unborn child. She seized the baby, held him close and fled downstairs in her nightdress.

She screamed for the melee to let her through. Still clutching the baby, she cradled her husband's dying head, letting his blood stain her nightdress.

'Husband! Ever my husband!' she whispered at his bloody body.

Buckingham opened his eyes wide at her as he died. He was thirty-five years old. Soubise then stood over him and whispered in his ear. Nobody caught what he said.

Charles had set up court at nearby East Meon, at the home of William Towerson. He had been intending to review the fleet that day, along with Phineas Pett. He was almost ready for departure when the terrible message came. Stiff faced and pale, he found Katherine holding baby George standing over Buckingham's body, which had been moved upstairs. Having satisfied himself that the cruel and unnatural perpetrator had been apprehended and was now in chains, he turned to Katherine.

'You will have my love and protection as long as we both live, dear Kate. And as to your son, who bears the beloved name, from this day he will be as my own flesh and blood.'

Katherine nodded, pale but calm. 'Thank you, Your Majesty.' And then the dam broke. 'O Charles, what a black, black day. How undeserved this is!'

They wept together. But they were among the few weeping for Buckingham.

The planned procession in state to burial at Westminster Abbey had to be carried out at night for fear of the mob. Charles had him laid to rest in the Henry VII chapel, usually reserved for those of royal blood. Here he would be near James, who had loved him too, in his own way.

But at the ceremony, soldiers under the command of the Lieutenant of the Tower refused to trail their pikes. They then refused an honour volley of shot before deserting with all the torches, leaving Buckingham to be buried in the dark.

Felton was taken to London and hanged. His body was taken back to Portsmouth and displayed as an object of opprobrium. But instead of that, the rotting corpse was treated as a place of pilgrimage as it swung from its gibbet on the beach. Le Sueur's bust of Charles on the Square Tower, on the other hand, was defaced and smeared with excrement.

Buckingham's memorial was the effigy on his tomb: The Enigma of the World. It was Charles's idea. With Henrietta's encouragement, her own playwright, James Shirley of the Queen's Men, wrote an encapsulated truth:

*Here lies the best and worst of fate*
*Two Kings' delight, the people's hate.*

Henrietta had realised her secret desire for the death of Buckingham. She had every hope of fully claiming her husband and monopolising his love.

The story continues in *The King's Art*, Novel 2 of the series *The Stuarts: Love, Art, War.*

# Author

Michael Dean has a history degree from Worcester College, Oxford, an MSc in Applied Linguistics from Edinburgh University and a translator's qualification (AIL) in German.

He has published several novels. *The Darkness into Light* omnibus (Sharpe Books, 2017), *The Rise and Fall of the Nazis* comprises five titles: *Before the Darkness* – about the German Jewish Foreign Minister Walther Rathenau, assassinated in 1922; *The Crooked Cross* – about Hitler and art; *The Enemy Within* – about Dutch resistance during the Nazi occupation; *Hour Zero* – about Germany in 1946; *Magic City* – a novel of Jewish identity set in Germany in the early 1970s.

He also published some stand-alone novels: *Thorn*, (Bluemoose Books, 2011) about Spinoza and Rembrandt; *I, Hogarth* (Duckworth-Overlook, 2012), which sets out to unify Hogarth's life with his art.

His novels, *The White Crucifixion*, about Marc Chagall, and *True Freedom*, or how America came to fight Britain for its independence, were published by Holland Park Press in 2018 and 2019.

His non-fiction includes a book about Chomsky and many educational publications.

Holland Park Press, founded in 2009, is a privately-owned independent company publishing literary fiction: novels, novellas, short stories; and poetry. The company is run by brother and sister team Arnold and Bernadette Jansen op de Haar, who publish an author not just a book. Holland Park Press specialises in finding new literary talent by accepting unsolicited manuscripts from authors all year round and by running competitions. It has been successful in giving older authors a chance to make their debut and in raising the profile of Dutch authors in translation.

To

Learn more about Michael Dean
Discover other interesting books
Read our blogs and news items
Find out how to submit your manuscript
Take part in one of our competitions

Visit www.hollandparkpress.co.uk

Bookshop: http://www.hollandparkpress.co.uk/books.php

Holland Park Press in the social media:

https://www.twitter.com/HollandParkPres
https://www.facebook.com/HollandParkPress
https://www.linkedin.com/company/holland-park-press
https://www.youtube.com/user/HollandParkPress
https://www.instagram.com/hollandparkpress/